**He prayed the kiss would tell him what he needed to know...**

And it did. Her mouth tasted the same as he'd remembered. Rich and inviting and unique to Sophia. But what was she doing here, in a bunker? Tipping his head, he changed the angle of contact, changed everything he'd thought was true.

Sophia Rhodes *was* here. And he was holding her.

Desperate to satisfy his craving, he slid one hand down her body, pulling her hips toward him. It seemed that time had reversed itself. They were back in the past together. Only this time he wasn't leaving in the morning. This time he'd keep her captive in his bed for days.

When he began to unbutton her shirt, she stiffened.

She pressed a finger to her lips. "Someone's coming!" She looked wildly around. "I've got to hide."

He didn't question her. The panic in her voice and on her face was enough to tell him she was in grave danger.

RUTH GLICK WRITING AS REBECCA YORK

# REBECCA YORK

# SOLDIER CAGED

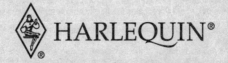

# HARLEQUIN®

TORONTO • NEW YORK • LONDON
AMSTERDAM • PARIS • SYDNEY • HAMBURG
STOCKHOLM • ATHENS • TOKYO • MILAN • MADRID
PRAGUE • WARSAW • BUDAPEST • AUCKLAND

To Norman, who always watches out for me.

ISBN-13: 978-0-373-69339-9
ISBN-10:      0-373-69339-7

SOLDIER CAGED

## ABOUT THE AUTHOR

Award-winning, bestselling novelist Ruth Glick, who writes as Rebecca York, is the author of more than 100 books, including her popular 43 Light Street series for Harlequin Intrigue. Ruth says she has the best job in the world. Not only does she get paid for telling stories, she's also the author of twelve cookbooks. Ruth and her husband, Norman, travel frequently, researching locales for her novels and searching out new dishes for her cookbooks.

## Books by Rebecca York

# CAST OF CHARACTERS

*Jonah Baker*—His life depended on sorting lies from reality.

*Sophia Rhodes*—How far would she go to help Jonah?

*Phil Martin*—Was he Sophia's friend or foe?

*Carlton Montgomery*—What did he want from Jonah?

*Colonel Luntz*—Was he working against Montgomery or with him?

*Lieutenant Calley*—Was he one of Montgomery's spies?

*Sergeant Henry*—Could he also be one of Montgomery's spies?

*Cameron Randolph*—Could Jonah trust him?

*Thorn Devereaux*—Could he provide the solution to Jonah's problem?

# Chapter One

Jonah Baker heard the chatter of a Kalashnikov, then another weapon returning fire. The sound was familiar in the craggy brown hills of a country where warlords ran rampant over the land, fighting each other for prestige and territory.

The sun played over the top of his helmet, and sweat crawled down his back under his flak jacket. For a man who'd grown up in… Grown up in…

He struggled to remember the place where he'd spent his childhood. He had to have come from *somewhere*. But he couldn't bring it into focus. Not the town. Not his house. Panic tightened his chest. Then he reminded himself that the past wasn't important right now. He had to focus on this village. These people.

They knew who had come here to harvest the viscous fluid from the immature poppy plants, then ship the darkened, slightly sticky mass called opium to middlemen.

He caught a flicker of movement to his right, but it was only a woman peering out from the doorway of her stone house.

Her whole body was hidden by a burka—a blue robe with a face screen that allowed her to view only a narrow slice of the world. But he saw her small hand clutching the wooden door frame. In her other hand she held a metal box with a crank. She let go of the woodwork and began to turn the crank. As she did, music started playing. It sounded foreign and exotic, something the men might dance to on a village feast day or at a wedding celebration. It should have been pleasant, but it sent shivers along his spine.

"Stop," he said, wanting to clamp his hands over his ears. "I mean you no harm," he added.

The woman eased back into the shadows beyond the doorway, but the tune kept grating at him until he strode away, scanning the street for trouble.

A few houses away, a group of men with dark beards, loose-fitting shirts, and colorful turbans stepped into view and stood facing the American soldiers. Some of them had lined, weather-worn faces that made them look as if they were in their seventies. But he suspected they were decades younger. Life in…

Again his mind drew a blank. And then it came to him. He was in Afghanistan. Tramping through the back of beyond, where there were no passable roads. Trying to cut off the source of funding for the Taliban.

"We won't punish you. We just want to know who harvested the opium," Lieutenant Calley said.

Calley?

Wasn't he someone from another conflict, decades ago?

"Damn," he muttered.

"Quiet. Don't interrupt," Calley ordered.

Jonah's head swung toward the man. "You don't give the orders. I'm the major. You're the lieutenant."

"But I'm better at the language. That's why I'm handling the questioning."

Jonah focused on the scene. Everything seemed normal. But something bad was going to happen. He felt it all the way to the marrow of his bones.

The villager doing the talking took a step back, his eyes darting away for a moment. "We don't know the men who came for the opium," he insisted.

"But you watched them work."

Somehow Jonah could understand perfectly what the guy was saying.

"There were a lot of them. They said they would kill us if we interfered."

"Uh-huh," Calley muttered.

Jonah saw him reach for his gun. "Don't!"

"I know how to get them to talk." Calley pulled out his sidearm and shot the old man.

A sick feeling rose in Jonah's throat. "What the hell are you doing?"

"Defending myself."

"No. You started it." Jonah backed away in horror. "Stop. Stop," he kept pleading, but Calley had gone mad.

He saw the woman in the doorway clutch her chest and fall. Red blood spread across her blue burka as she lay on the ground.

A bullet slammed into his thigh and he went down. Then another one caught him in the arm.

Horror swirled through his mind, through his soul. He was still screaming "No" when his eyes opened and he found himself lying on a narrow bed in a darkened room.

Sweat drenched his skin and the T-shirt and briefs he was wearing. The bedclothes were tangled around him. Dim light filtered in under the crack at the bottom of the door.

He'd awakened from a nightmare—about Afghanistan. His last assignment.

He pressed the heels of his hands against his eyes.

No, he corrected himself immediately. That wasn't his last assignment.

The dream was so vivid, that it had seemed like reality. But he knew he had made it up. It wasn't real. Lieutenant Calley was a soldier from Vietnam, notorious for having ordered the mass murder of innocent villagers. That was how he had ended up in a nightmare about the massacre of a village in the Afghan hills.

Or was there something real about the dream—and his mind had twisted the facts? Like the lieutenant's name.

He moved his arm and found it was sore, as though he'd suffered a recent injury. Fumbling beside the bed, he found a table and a lamp attached to the wall. He switched on the lamp, then sat blinking in the sudden light.

When his vision cleared, he looked at the upper part of his right arm and saw a round red scar from a recent bullet wound.

Like in the dream.

And what about his leg?

Quickly he pulled the covers aside and found another scar on his right thigh. Just where he'd been hit in the nightmare village.

So where was he now?

Was this a prison? An asylum?

Once again, panic gripped his throat and he pushed himself off the bed because he needed to get away from the place where the dream had grabbed him.

When he stood up, pain shot through his injured thigh. He caught his breath, adjusted the weight on the leg, then staggered to the door.

To his vast relief, when he turned the knob, the door opened.

Thank God. At least he wasn't locked in. He stared down a long corridor, lit only by dim emergency lights. Like those in his room, the walls were of cinder block painted an institutional green. And the lights were spaced about every fifteen feet, leaving pools of darkness between them.

If he had to guess, he'd say it was night, and they'd turned the lights down because most people were sleeping. Or maybe that was the norm in this place.

He closed the door and leaned against it, trying to bring the recent past into focus.

He felt a wave of relief when details came zinging back to him. He'd been in Thailand. *That* was his last assignment.

Images flooded his mind. Beautiful gold-and-red temples. Fifteen-foot-high statues of Buddha. Lotus blossoms. Peaked roofs so different from the architecture of any other country he had visited. A wide river where fantailed outboard motorboats zipped past each other. Streets clogged with cars and trucks and little three-wheeled open-air cabs with a driver on something like a motorcycle in the front and a bench seat in the back for the passengers.

He'd taken those cabs. And he'd ridden on an elephant, feeling as though he was going to fall off the bench seat swaying on top of the lumbering beast.

Yeah, Thailand. But what was he doing there?

Once he had the name of the country and remembered some of the things he'd seen and done, the answer supplied itself. He'd been working security for a diplomatic mission to Bangkok. The diplomats wanted to see the ancient capital of Ayutthaya, burned by the Burmese two hundred years ago. The stone buildings were still standing, like ghosts of their former selves.

But while the party was away from the city, they got word that bird flu had broken out in the area. A deadly airborne strain. And the only sure way to avoid getting infected was to go underground—into a secret bunker.

As news of the epidemic had spread, panicked citizens had attacked them, trying to get to safety. That's where he'd gotten shot, defending the diplomats. He remembered that very clearly now.

He closed his eyes for a moment, trying to come up with more details. They evaded him.

But he knew he'd made it to safety.

In the bunker?

A secret bunker in Thailand?

Yeah, the U.S. government had dug them for the king at various locations around the country. Or that was the story. What else would they be for?

He looked around the little room. It was maybe seven by ten feet, just big enough for a single bed, a night table bolted to the wall and a small chest of drawers. Besides the door to the hall, there were two others. When he checked them, he found a shallow closet where uniform pants and shirts hung. Not his usual uniform. These were navy blue.

The bunker uniform?

He had some vague memory of having someone strip off his clothing, then take him through a special biological decontamination area. When he came out and dried off, he was issued all new clothing.

He kept moving along the wall and found that the other door led to a small bathroom. Switching on the light, he looked around and saw a toilet, sink and narrow shower stall.

On the shelf over the sink were toiletries, including a tube of toothpaste that was half used up. How long had he been here?

A time frame came to him. Three weeks. He'd been here healing and waiting out the epidemic.

They'd separated the security detail from the diplomats. He remembered that now. And Dr. Montgomery was in charge of this section of the bunker.

So the story about Afghanistan was something he'd made up, a dream. Or had that happened, too, farther back in his past?

He ran a shaky hand over his face, as though that would clear his mind. It didn't help. But at least he could use logic. If he'd been part of a village massacre in Afghanistan, he'd hardly be the choice for a diplomatic mission. Probably he'd be in the brig instead.

Maybe he could ask Dr. Montgomery about that. The name brought back vague memories of being in the doctor's office. Not for medical treatment. The man was a psychologist or something like that, and he was supposed to be helping Jonah cope with post-traumatic stress.

Except that Jonah didn't trust the guy, even when he kept saying what sounded like the right things.

So did that make Jonah Baker paranoid?

He leaned over the sink, staring at his reflection in the mirror. At least he recognized the man who stared back, although he got the impression from the lean look of his face that he'd lost some weight in the past few weeks.

Picking up the glass from the shelf above the sink, he filled it from the tap and took several swallows of cold water. Then he turned off the bathroom light and went back to the twin bed, where he straightened the covers again, tucking in the bottom corners with military precision.

The pillow was half off the bed, and he saw something that had been under it. A pill.

What the hell was a pill doing there?

Wait a minute. It was something he was supposed to take. Only it had made his head fuzzy. So when the sergeant had given it to him, he'd pretended to swallow it. Then he'd spat it out and tucked it under his pillow.

But what was he thinking? He couldn't leave it there. With a dart of panic, he grabbed it and flushed it down the toilet. Climbing back under the covers, he turned off the bedside lamp and tried to go back to sleep. Instead he lay there staring into the darkness, unanswered questions swirling in his mind.

As he listened to the sound of his own breathing, a noise riveted his attention.

Focusing intently, he thought he heard the knob turn. Then the door opened just far enough for someone to slip into the room before it closed again. Someone who assumed Jonah Baker was sleeping and they could sneak around without him being the wiser. So what the hell was the intruder up to?

Too bad Jonah hadn't checked the quarters for a weapon. He had nothing but his hands—and surprise—to defend himself. For the moment, all he could do was remain very still, feigning sleep. He heard the sound of harsh breathing.

So the guy was nervous.

Was he planning to shoot the sleeping man? No. He could have done that already. So maybe he had a knife? That would certainly attract less attention.

When the assailant came softly across the floor, Jonah forced himself to stay where he was. He'd been shot recently, so he wasn't exactly in top fighting form. But in the dim light, this guy looked small, and maybe Jonah could take him.

As a hand reached out, Jonah made his move—springing up and grabbing the outstretched arm, twisting it over and back.

The guy tried to cry out, but Jonah clamped a hand across the man's mouth, pulling him back against his own body.

"Call for help and I'll kill you," he rasped.

Still holding the arm in a grip that would dislocate the guy's shoulder if he moved the wrong way, Jonah slid his other hand downward, searching for weapons.

He didn't find a knife or a gun.

Instead his hand closed over a woman's breast.

## Chapter Two

"Jonah, don't."

She spoke as though she knew him well, and the mingling of fear and determination in her voice was like a punch in the gut.

"You're hurting my arm. Let me go."

He eased up a little, but he didn't loosen his hold on her. "Who are you? What are you doing here?"

In the darkness, he heard her swallow hard. "I'm Sophia. Sophia Rhodes."

He hadn't expected to hear a name he recognized. But the effect was that of a baseball bat to the chest, knocking the breath from his lungs.

A few minutes ago, he had remembered nothing about his early life. But the mention of her name sent a bolt of lightning through his brain. The lightning crashed through a mental barrier, releasing a dam of memories into his mind. Not just memories. Vivid physical sensations.

He remembered a night in her bed. A night of passionate kisses and touches. And then two bodies joined in ecstasy and desperation. A night that had branded him for life.

He summoned the breath to speak and managed to gasp, "You can't be."

"I am," she answered, her tone almost as breathy as his, making him wonder if the same memories had flashed through her consciousness and affected her the same way.

Shock made his muscles go weak, and his hold on her loosened. With a small sound, she pulled away.

"It's me," she said. "See for yourself."

Bending down, she turned on the light above the bedside table, and he thought with one corner of his mind that she knew just where to find the switch. He blinked, fighting the sudden brightness as he struggled to focus on her.

She was dressed in a uniform identical to the ones that hung in the closet. Only she had added a cap with a visor. When she pulled the cap off, a cloud of glorious wheat-colored hair fell around her shoulders.

His hand remembered the feel of that hair. Unable to stop himself, he reached out, running his fingers through the wavy strands, letting them tangle in the softness.

In the dark he had assumed she was a man. Now he was confounded that he could have made such a mistake.

Her large blue eyes searched his face, then slid lower—over his almost naked body.

Earlier he'd felt at a disadvantage, lying in bed waiting for some guy to assault him. Now the sensation was multiplied as he stood facing Sophia. But he held his ground, taking in the details of her. She still had the same delicate features. The little turned-up nose that he had found so enchanting. The bee-stung lips. The high cheekbones. The creamy skin that burned when she tried to get a tan.

Too bad he couldn't see the mark that might confirm her identity—the little brown imperfection high up on her right thigh, just below her butt. With an effort, he pulled his mind away from that spot and studied her face again.

She'd been nineteen and back from her first year at a posh eastern college when they'd made love. He had been a couple of years older—because he'd been kept back early in his school career when he'd had trouble learning to read. Then there'd been the year he'd bummed around before he'd let an army recruiter convince him that serving his country was his ticket out of a dead-end life like his mom and dad's.

This woman was definitely older than the girl he remembered. Probably about ten years older. But maturity hadn't made her less appealing to him. There was wisdom in her eyes now. Or was it calculation? He hated to think of her in those terms. In his memory she'd been the goddess who'd starred in the most satisfying and yet the most gut-wrenching night of his life.

But maybe she wasn't Sophia Rhodes. How could it be? How could she have found him? More to the point, how could she have gotten into this bunker in Thailand?

He hated standing in front of her wearing only a pair of revealing briefs when she was fully dressed.

Taking the chance on turning his back, he walked to the closet and grabbed a pair of uniform pants off a hanger. Then he pulled them on, wincing as he lifted his right leg and shoved it into the pants.

While he performed the simple task, his mind was racing. Who was she, really? What if someone had found a woman who looked like Sophia Rhodes, used plastic surgery to make her into an exact double and sent her to him?

And why go to all that trouble to fool Major Jonah Baker?

After zipping the fly, he turned back to her.

"You hurt your leg," she whispered.

"I'll live."

"What happened?"

"I got shot when…" He stopped as warring images clashed

inside his head. "When we were running for the bunker," he finished, watching her face.

She looked concerned for him. But why not? If someone had sent Sophia Rhodes or her double to get information from him, of course she'd act concerned. She'd want him to think she was on his side—whatever that meant.

So was she an enemy agent?

He didn't want to believe that scenario—or anything else bad of her. But, under the circumstances, bad was more likely than good.

His throat was so tight he couldn't speak at the moment. Struggling to conquer his wildly swinging emotions, he studied her face, trying not to react to his memories of the woman or the surge of need that rushed through him. Not just physical need. Something much more profound and much more dangerous.

Ruthlessly, he stiffened his resolve, although he hoped that didn't show on his face.

But he knew he must be alert for any lies she was planning to tell him. "How could you be here? Have you been here the whole time, or did you slip into the bunker somehow?"

She ignored the questions and simply said, "I came to help you."

"Came to Thailand?"

She made a strangled sound. "That's where they said you are?"

"What do you mean? It's not what they *said*. It's true."

Even as he mouthed the denial, he felt a worm of doubt slithering down his spine. He had pictures in his mind of Thailand. Temples. Elephants. An ancient ruined city. Vendors lining the streets.

But sometimes it felt as though he was watching a Power Point presentation as he brought up each scene in his memory.

She must have read the expression on his face. "It's okay. Don't worry about where we are."

"I have to worry about it," he ground out. "It's my job."

"I understand," she answered much too quickly.

He matched her reaction time. "Do you?"

"Yes," she whispered, reaching out her hands and gently clasping his arms. He might have wrenched away. Instead, he went very still. Dragging in a breath, he caught the scent of honey and herbs. His memory didn't associate that combination with her. When he'd known her before, she'd smelled of lemon.

He ordered himself to stop focusing on her fragrance.

Through parched lips, he said, "If you're Sophia Rhodes, tell me something we would both remember."

His heart was pounding as he waited for her to mention the night they'd spent together. Instead she said, "Do you remember Mrs. Watson?"

As he scrambled to bring the name into context, she went on.

"The Latin teacher. We used to say her boobs hung down so low that her belt held them up."

At the image, he couldn't keep a bark of a laugh from escaping. He hadn't remembered that on his own, but now it zinged back to him.

"She'd walk around the room, and you wouldn't know who she was going to call on for a translation of Caesar's *Gallic Wars*. I used to do the homework and translate the chapters every night. But you hated the assignments. You used a pony. You remember?"

Ah, the cheat book. He remembered it well. "Yeah."

"But there were certain words—like *corn* instead of *grain*—that would give you away. If you used the wrong word—the one in the pony—you'd get an F for the day."

"Yeah," he said again. Just an hour ago, his early life had been a big fat blank, but now he remembered hating Latin class. He'd be sitting there across the room from the big clock on the wall. Every time a minute passed, the big hand would move and make a clicking sound. And he'd watch it, praying that it would move around to the time for the bell to ring before the old witch called on him. Sometimes she was in the mood to torture him. And sometimes she let him alone. He'd never known from day to day which it would be.

"Why did you take Latin," she asked, "if you didn't want to do the work?"

"I don't know," he answered, feeling an inward stab. That was a lie. He'd taken it because Sophia was in the class.

To change the subject, he demanded, "Tell me something else."

Partly he was testing her, and partly he was testing himself. Because when she spoke, she brought scenes and people back to him.

"You and Roger Berg and Kevin Drake used to sit at table twenty-two in the cafeteria. All of you wore black T-shirts and faded jeans with holes in the knees. And you'd decide which guys could sit with you. But they had to be tough enough. Didn't Tony Swazey steal a GPS from a car to prove he was up to your standards? Only the cops caught him and he ended up in reform school?"

"I never told Tony Swazey to steal anything!"

"But he did it to prove that he was good enough to sit with you."

"Not my fault."

She caught her breath, and he wondered what she was thinking.

"What?" he asked, watching her closely.

She swallowed. "You know he's dead?"

Jonah's stomach clenched. "Yeah. He was in a helicopter crash in Iraq."

"Yes."

Another memory. That one from after he'd left… He wanted to ask her the name of the town where they'd gone to school, but he didn't want to give that much away.

She was speaking again. "You remember the drama club production of *Bye Bye Birdy?* You were Birdy and I was one of the screaming girls who idolized you."

Yeah, he remembered that. The part had been perfect for him.

Sophia had deliberately dragged his mind away from the death of Tony Swazey. But he was tired of playing the game by the rules she'd set up. Or maybe he was tired of her talking about the time when he'd been unsure of himself with her. He wanted to leap past that period in his life to something a lot more satisfactory. But he wasn't going to be the one to bring up that night.

"Stop talking about the high-school scene," he growled. "Tell me something about us."

He saw her swallow again.

"Okay. We liked each other. We used to watch each other across the room and in the halls. My girlfriends used to tease me about you. But neither one of us had the guts to cross that gap—until that night."

"That night," he repeated, relieved that she'd finally brought it out into the open. "Go on."

"I went to that bar to meet—"

"A guy named Kip Weld," he finished the sentence for her. "Only he never showed up. And I stopped some ratty-looking moron from hitting on you."

She kept her gaze steady. "Actually, I was lying. I was there to meet *you*. I made up the Kip Weld story."

He stared at her, thunderstruck.

It flashed into his mind that the time for lying had passed—about that night and about what was happening now. He had to know if she spoke the truth.

Reaching out, he cupped his hands over her shoulders. Her blue eyes went wide as he drew her close, swaying her body against his.

He stopped looking into her eyes as he lowered his mouth to

hers. Moving slowly, he wrapped his arms around her so that he flattened her breasts against his chest.

He cursed the uniform shirt and bra that denied him the intimate contact he craved.

Still, the pressure went straight from his chest to his groin. He clung to her as a whirlwind of sensations swamped him. The brush of her corn-silk hair against his cheek. The way her body pressed to his. The enveloping honey-spice scent.

Too dizzy to stand on his own, he took a step back, bringing her with him as he braced his hips against the wall. The earth was tilting under his feet, and he fought to anchor himself.

She swayed, her arms reaching up to circle his neck.

He moved his lips against hers, brushing, sliding, settling. His tongue stroked along the seam, asking her to open for him.

Without hesitation, she did, and he played with the line of her teeth, then dipped farther into her warmth, tasting her fully, completely.

It wasn't pure lust that motivated him, although that was certainly part of it. He had been holding his breath, praying that the kiss would tell him what he needed to know—about her and about himself.

And it did—as far as her identity was concerned. Her mouth had the same taste he had remembered on so many lonely nights. Rich and inviting and unique to Sophia.

She made a small sound that zinged along his nerve endings. He needed more, so much more. Tipping his head first one way and then the other, he changed the angle of contact, changed everything that he had thought was true.

He hadn't believed that Sophia Rhodes could be in this place. At this time.

But it was her. Holding her and touching her confirmed that on a very basic level.

One part of his mind was amazed that they had gone from interrogation to intimacy in seconds. But why should he be surprised? He had made love with her on one mind-blowing night, and for ten years, he had wanted more.

Desperate to satisfy his craving for erotic contact with her, he slid one hand down her body, pulling her hips against his erection, sorry now that he had put on his pants.

She moaned, moving against him, telling him she was as frustrated as he was by the layers of clothing that separated his skin from hers.

He was trembling as he slipped a hand between them, cupping one of her breasts, then stroking his fingers across the hardened crest.

"Oh!" she exclaimed, the word going directly into his greedy mouth.

It seemed that time had stood still or reversed itself. They were back in the past together. Only this time he wasn't leaving in the morning. This time he would keep her captive in his bed for days.

She was his. Totally his. He knew that without a sliver of doubt.

When he began to unbutton her shirt, she eased far enough away to give him access. Dipping his head, he buried his face in the valley between her breasts, and she cupped her hands around the back of his head.

Then, all at once, she stiffened. When she pushed against his shoulder, he blinked.

"You don't want—?"

She pressed a finger against her lips. "Someone's coming."

His senses had contracted to a narrow focus—the woman in his arms. Now they expanded again, and he heard footsteps coming down the hall.

She looked wildly around. "I've got to hide."

He didn't question her. The panic in her voice and on her face was enough to tell him she was in grave danger. And it sounded as if they had only seconds to get her to safety.

He dragged her across the room. Turning off the light, he threw the covers aside as he pushed her onto the bed, then came down on top of her, lying facedown, and pulled the covers up. Then he lay still, pretending that he was the only occupant of the room.

The door opened, and he tried to look like a man who was sleeping.

Jonah's back was to the door, but through slitted eyes, he saw the play of a flashlight on the wall. When it shifted to his body, he felt Sophia stiffen and knew she saw it too.

He tensed, readying himself to leap out of bed and assault whoever had invaded his space.

## Chapter Three

As Sophia waited to find out what would happen, contingency plans raced through her head.

Centuries dragged by as the guard—it had to be one of the guards—inspected the room and lingered in the doorway. What if he found her here? How was she going to explain what she was doing in Jonah's room? In his bed, no less.

She'd had a cover story. Now it seemed ridiculous that she could be here as part of an oversight team to make sure Montgomery was doing his job. But that was the best she had.

To conquer her fear, she tried to focus on Jonah. The physical sensations would have swamped her, if she didn't have something else to worry about. She could feel Jonah's chest through her uniform shirt. Feel his broad shoulders and his hard thighs.

He was giving a good imitation of a man sleeping, his breath deep and even. But she knew from the tension in his arms and shoulders that he was ready to spring up if the guard came closer.

Long seconds ticked by. Finally the invader backed up and closed the door, and she heard footsteps continue down the hall.

She let out the breath she'd been holding, then pressed a hand against Jonah's shoulder. "You're crushing me."

"Sorry." He rolled to the side, keeping his arm across her middle. "You know who that was?"

"The guards here make random checks. Don't you remember seeing any of them before?"

He made a frustrated sound. "No."

"You're having trouble with your memory?"

Instead of giving her a straight answer, he asked, "Why do you think so?"

She wasn't sure how to respond. She didn't want to alarm him any more than she had to. Not yet. But she knew saying too much or too little could get them both killed.

Before she decided how much to tell him, he asked another question—this one more direct. "Are we in Thailand?"

His voice was full of urgency. But the only answer she could give him was, "I can't tell you."

His hand tightened on her waist. "Can't or won't?"

"It's not a good idea."

"Why the hell not?"

"Because it's better if they think you believe what they told you."

He muttered a curse.

To give him another focus and because she needed to know the answer, she asked, "What do you remember about the days just before you came here?"

He rolled to his back and pulled his arm away, and she breathed a small sigh, relieved that they were no longer lying quite so intimately. The contact made it hard to think. Still, in the narrow bed, there was no way to get much distance from him.

In the dark, she reached into her pocket, then slid her hand down beside the bed, her knuckles hitting one of the slats.

"What was that?"

"My arm slipped off the bed."

In the darkness, she could see only Jonah's profile, but she remembered how he had looked at her a few minutes ago. The image merged and shifted, overlaid with her memories of him.

Ten years ago he'd worn his dark hair a little too long. Now, of course, it was much shorter. Probably it had been military length, but it had grown out in the weeks he'd been here. His eyes were the same. Those dark eyes that she'd always thought could see right into her head. The blade of a nose. The strong jaw. The lean hips.

She pulled her mind back from below his waist and focused on his profile.

It looked as though he was staring up into the darkness. Finally, he said, "You're really Sophia."

She breathed out a small sigh. At least they'd gotten that far. "Yes."

"What are you doing here?"

"I already answered that. I came to help you."

"Help me do what?"

"Stay alive."

He made a small sound in his throat. "How?"

She came back to a previous question, approaching it in a different way. "You said you were in Thailand. What were you doing there?"

"I was part of a security detail guarding diplomats. They went on a sightseeing trip to some ruins. We were supposed to come back to Bangkok by boat, but we got caught in a bird-flu epidemic."

"And how did you end up in this place? What is it?"

"A former fallout shelter built for the king. But it's sealed, so it keeps us safe from the flu."

*A clever story. Very realistic,* she thought. *So how did I get in?* She kept that question to herself because she didn't want to end up supplying an answer.

"So you remember Thailand." She dragged in a breath and let it out slowly. "But what about Afghanistan?"

He turned toward her, his voice suddenly harsh. "How do you know about that?"

She clenched her fist, her nails digging into her palm. She'd been briefed, but she wasn't sure how much to tell him. Or what information would make him trust her and what would make him sure that she was the enemy. Despite the passionate kiss, she knew he had to be worried about that. And she could only go so far with reassuring him.

"Tell me what you remember about Afghanistan," she demanded, pushing him a little.

"I'm not sure how accurate it is. I dreamed about it. It can't be real, though. I mean, in the dream, Lieutenant Calley was one of the men with me. And he was in the Vietnam War, wasn't he?"

"Yes. But that doesn't make the dream totally wrong."

"Great! Thanks."

Ignoring the sarcasm in his voice, she asked, "A Dr. Montgomery has been questioning you?" Her breath stilled as she waited for his answer. She needed to confirm that the information she'd been given was correct, but she hated the idea of Jonah in Montgomery's clutches after what she'd read about the man. He was an expert interrogator, skilled in the use of intimidation, behavior modification techniques and drugs. And when those methods didn't achieve the desired effects, he'd been known to use torture.

"He's helping me deal with post-traumatic stress."

"Did he prescribe medication?"

He didn't answer for long moments. Finally, he said, "Yes."

"Stop taking it."

"What if I…need it?"

"You don't," she said, trying to make her voice authoritative. "Stop taking it. That will help you sort out your memories."

His voice turned hard and urgent. "How do you know?"

"I was told."

"By whom?"

"Let's get back to Montgomery. He's asking you questions, right?"

"Yeah."

"Don't tell him anything about Afghanistan," she said, hearing the plea in her own voice.

"Why not?"

"Because the moment he gets what he wants out of you, you're expendable."

He made a sound that could have been a harsh laugh. "That's just great."

"Don't forget that. He'll act like he's your friend, but you mustn't trust him."

He raised up, his face inches from hers. "Did you really come here just to talk?"

Before she could figure out how to answer, he rolled toward her again and wrapped his arms around her, pulling her tight against his body.

Apparently he'd thought of a more pleasurable activity than their disturbing conversation.

She knew she should push away from him, but she craved the contact as much as he did. When he tipped her chin up, she was helpless to do anything besides let him bring his mouth back to hers for another searing kiss.

There was only one man who had kissed her like that, and it was Jonah Baker. And then he had walked away.

Of course, he hadn't wanted to. She had comforted herself with that undeniable truth. He'd been scheduled to report to boot camp. Still, he could have made an effort to contact her after basic training.

She'd waited weeks to hear from him, and she'd been devastated that he hadn't called. Later, she'd thought maybe she should have reached out to him, but she'd been too proud and too hurt to ask why he'd walked away from what they'd found together. And too immature and unsure of herself to go after what she so desperately wanted.

None of that had stopped her from volunteering for this assignment—even when they'd laid out all the details so she would know the danger involved.

Maybe she secretly thought this was her second chance. She wasn't going to blow it this time.

She didn't want to think about her motives too deeply. Not now. Instead, she focused on the kiss, letting it consume her.

A few minutes ago, he'd been the aggressor. This time she gave as good as she got, feasting from his lips, then deepening the kiss, her tongue exploring his mouth the way he'd explored hers and sliding tantalizingly against his tongue.

She couldn't see him with the light off, but she reached out to touch his face, stroking her fingers over the familiar contours of his brows, his cheeks, his nose.

She felt him smile against her mouth, then turn his head so he could nibble at her earlobe, then her jaw and finally her throat. So he remembered how much she liked that!

She arched her neck, his lips on her there making her as hot as the mouth-to-mouth contact.

He nibbled with his teeth at her sensitive skin, then soothed her with his tongue. At the same time, she felt his fingers on the top button of her shirt. Once again, he slipped it open, then the next one, so that he could bury his face between her breasts. He turned his head to kiss first one inner curve and then the other.

At the same time, he shifted his position so that his erection was pressed to the cleft at the juncture of her legs.

And that felt so good.

She stifled a cry, loving what he was doing, loving the heat blazing up inside her. Yet she knew that if she gave herself over to the man and the pleasure, she could be steering them both to disaster.

She had to be the one in control. The one whose sound judgment would get them out of this trap.

With the last shred of her resolve, she slipped from his grasp and rolled away from him, then sprang off the bed, standing on legs that barely held her weight. When she backed up and stepped on something soft, she jumped, then realized it was her cap. Sweeping her hair into a quick twist, she shoved it under the protective covering. Still shaky, she buttoned her shirt, then moved back so that her shoulder was leaning against the wall.

"Sophia?" His voice sounded so raw that she almost came back to the bed.

But she stayed where she was. "We can't. You know it's too dangerous. Neither one of us can afford to stop thinking straight."

"But you wanted me?"

"Do you really have to ask?"

"I want to hear you say it."

"You know I did. Yes. I wanted you."

He huffed out a breath, then climbed off the bed. When he stepped toward her, she moved farther along the wall.

With a shaky finger, she pressed the button on her watch, lighting the dial so she could look at the time.

"It's three-eighteen. The guard could be coming back, and I have to get out of here before he does."

"Or what?"

"Let's just say it's a lot better for both of us if I don't get caught."

"So you admit you're here illegally."

"You could put it that way."

"How would *you* put it?"

"I've already said what I can. I have to leave, but I'll be back. Just don't talk about Afghanistan."

"Am I in prison?"

"No!"

"Then what?"

She felt her throat tighten. "Just play your cards close to your chest, okay?"

His voice turned gritty. "If I'm in so much trouble here, take me with you now."

Her throat constricted even more, so that she was barely able to speak. "I can't. Not yet."

He exploded with a string of curses that tore at her resolve.

"Jonah, please!"

She couldn't see his face, but she felt him glaring at her. "You come here like…like a thief, and you expect me to go for this crap? You have to give me more information if you want me to go along with you!"

Her insides clenched. "Jonah, I'm sorry."

"Just give me a straight answer. Why can't I leave now?"

She closed her eyes for a moment, then opened them again. "Your leg."

"What about it?"

"The route out of here isn't easy. You have to be in better shape."

He cursed again.

She pushed the light on her watch once more, not just to see the time. She wanted to make the point that she couldn't stand here arguing with him any longer.

"I have to go."

"Yeah, go on."

The bruised tone of his voice made her stomach knot so tightly that she almost doubled over in pain.

She lingered, pushing her luck because she wanted to take him in her arms and reassure him. And she had one more thing to do. Crossing the room, she opened the closet.

"What are you doing?"

"Making sure I'll recognize you." Quickly she stooped down, found his shoes and stuck a small monitor under the flap where the tongue was attached.

"Everybody wears the same thing."

She stood. "I see." It was a nonsense reply but it was the best she could do. "I'll be back."

"When?" he asked, as if he thought the answer was going to be a lie.

"I can't tell you exactly."

"Sure."

She pressed her hand against her stomach, trying to hold back the pain that twisted in her gut. She had known this would be difficult, but she'd had no idea how difficult emotionally.

She'd been so hopeful when she came in. But now she knew that she'd been feeling what she wanted to feel.

Seeing him again. Touching him. Kissing him. Lying to him. The combination was devastating.

Turning quickly, she opened the door.

She didn't look back, but she knew that every fiber of Jonah's attention was focused on her.

Thankfully, she saw that the hallway was empty, so she exited quickly, then sprinted down the corridor.

WHEN THE DOOR closed, Jonah clenched his hands at his sides. He wanted to charge down the corridor after Sophia, though he wasn't even sure why. Did he want to shake her and scream at her, or beg for her help? Probably he couldn't even catch her, because of his damn leg.

She was right about that. He couldn't move fast. So what was she saying about the route out? It wasn't the elevator that he remembered?

Was he remembering it wrong? Or maybe they couldn't use the elevator, and he was going to have to climb an endless stairway. Well, good luck with that!

He clenched his right hand into a fist and pounded against his left palm, frustration surging through him.

He didn't know whether to trust her or go find the guards and tell them somebody had broken into this place.

No. He canceled that thought. He didn't want her to get hurt.

For old times' sake? Or because of how their bodies had responded to each other?

She could have been faking arousal. But he didn't think so. Still, if he believed what she had told him, he was in deep kimchi.

Well, it seemed as though he'd already been thinking that. Apparently, he'd decided not to take his damn pills.

He sat down on the side of the bed, leaning over and cradling his head in his hands.

Sophia had accomplished two things during her brief stay. She had brought back buried memories, and she'd made him think about this place and the people. The latter impressions were still vague. He could barely remember anything besides this room. He must have been walking around like a zombie. A chemically induced zombie.

He felt a cold chill go through him. What was he taking, exactly? Was that why his memories were cloudy? Skipping one pill was making them better? Or had he skipped more?

He couldn't remember. But that still left the question of Sophia. Friend or foe?

He didn't have enough information to figure it out.

He lay down, stacking his hands behind his head and thinking about his life before this place. At least her visit had given him some glimpses into his past. They had talked about high school, and she hadn't mentioned where it was. But he knew now. Ellicott City, Maryland.

They'd gone to Centennial High on Centennial Lane. She'd lived in one of the big new houses that were going up in Howard County. He'd lived in a dinky apartment across from Chatham Mall.

The familiar names gave him something to grasp on to. And also made his stomach clench.

He remembered the kid he'd been back then. A lanky teenager, standing tall even with the enormous chip he was carrying around on his shoulder. So many of the kids who went to school with him had all the money they wanted, lived in McMansions, and drove late-model cars, while he and his mom were crammed into a tiny apartment that was one step up from a housing project. His transportation was a clunker that he worked on himself in the parking lot of the rental complex.

The only reason Mom could afford the place was because of Section Eight—rent assistance—and food stamps.

They'd been okay when Dad was alive. He'd had a dead-end job in a warehouse, but at least he'd brought home a steady paycheck.

But he'd died in a car wreck when Jonah was twelve, and Mom didn't have the education to get a good-paying job. She'd worked fast food or in the service department of a car dealership. Sometimes one in the day and the other in the evening.

More details of his life were coming back—and they were ones he'd rather forget.

When he'd been old enough to get a job at a fast-food restaurant, he'd kept the money for himself. The memory made him cringe, because he understood now that he should have contributed some of it to their living expenses. But with the logic of a juvenile jerk, he'd figured he deserved some of what the other kids had. The only way to get it was to pay for it out of his earnings. Or steal it.

Yeah. He'd done some shoplifting back then. Mostly at the upscale mall in Columbia.

He whistled through his teeth. No wonder he didn't want to remember his misguided youth.

But the present wasn't much better.

Let's see. What did he know?

He ticked off the facts on his hands.

He was stuck in a secure facility. He'd thought he was here to rehabilitate. Now, from what Sophia had said, it looked as though this was a carefully controlled environment designed to extract information.

From him.

And mind-altering drugs were part of the package.

He didn't really know how long he'd been here. Maybe it was three weeks. Maybe not. He couldn't trust his memory. And a woman from his past had showed up to warn him not to trust his doctor.

He shuddered. How was that for a paranoid scenario? He wanted to stride down the hall, find someone in charge and demand answers about what was really going on in this place— wherever it was. But he suspected it was dangerous to do something outside the pattern they were expecting.

Still, in the morning, he was going to start taking charge of his life again.


SOPHIA HURRIED along the corridor, keeping her head down, even though she wanted to glance up at the security cameras.

They were supposed to be off, but she wasn't going to take a chance on getting her face photographed in case the jamming device had malfunctioned.

Her senses were on alert. This was no place to lose your focus. She wasn't supposed to be here, and if someone caught her, she'd have to go into her song and dance about a surprise inspection—and pray that the story would hold up long enough for her to figure out a way to escape.

At all costs, she couldn't let them know that she had come here to talk to Jonah.

Her heart squeezed when she thought about their meeting. She wanted to think that it had gone really well with him, that they'd connected on a very basic level. In truth, however, because she hadn't been able to tell him much, she'd made him wary. As he should be, unfortunately.

Did he believe her enough to keep his mouth shut with Montgomery?

She prayed she'd gotten that through to him. And prayed that she could get out of here without being seen.

Starting to turn a corner, she saw a man in a blue uniform coming toward her and stopped dead in her tracks.

One of the guards.

Backing up, she turned and ran along the hallway, hoping she could make it to safety before the guy discovered there was an intruder in the facility.

# Chapter Four

Sophia zipped around a corner.

As part of her training for the mission, she'd gone over and over the plans for this bunker. It was vast, and she knew there were places she could hide—if she could get to one.

The corridor walls were cinder-block. The first door she came to was locked. The second one, too. She wanted to look over her shoulder, but that would slow her down, and the guy behind her might see her face.

She reached a door marked Danger High Voltage. This time, when she tried the knob, it turned. She slipped into a darkened room, listening for the hum of electrical equipment. She heard nothing. Was this really part of the electrical plant? She couldn't remember. But she knew that if she bumped into a transformer, she was a cooked goose.

She could feel her heart pounding as she retrieved the small flashlight from her pocket. The narrow beam showed her only a small area at one time. Most of the room was still swathed in darkness.

Behind her, out in the corridor, she thought she heard footsteps.

There was no time to plan anything tricky. All she could do was slide along the wall and press herself into the shadows where the guy's line of sight would be blocked when the door opened. She killed the light and waited with her pulse pounding, clutching her flashlight handle. It had Mace in it—her only weapon. She'd drawn the line at killing anyone when she came in here.

The door opened and a powerful beam swept the room. But the man didn't step inside and look behind the door. After long seconds, the door closed again, and she breathed a sigh of relief.

She stayed put for several minutes, then pressed her ear to the barrier. When she detected nothing, she turned the knob and peered out.

Thankfully, she saw that the hallway was empty and she didn't hear any alarm bells. She reasoned that the guard hadn't really seen her; he was just following his rounds. Now, however, she was headed in the wrong direction; she could easily bump into another guard coming on shift.

Forcing herself not to run, she headed back the way she'd come. When she reached the cross corridor, she turned right, then took a flight of stairs down into the lower reaches of the facility, where she passed rooms with enormous tanks for water and fuel. The storeroom she wanted was about a hundred yards from the stairway.

Stepping inside, she played her light over shelves with boxes of canned fruit, pork and beans, tomato sauce, toilet paper, soap.

She was almost home free.

Unable to stop herself from running, she sprinted to the back and squeezed behind a line of shelves, where she pressed on a panel in the wall. It slid back, revealing a hidden doorway.

She stepped through, and ducked around a rock wall, then said a little prayer of thanksgiving that she'd made it out of the bunker in one piece.

She'd exited through the back door—a door she'd been told the men using the place didn't know existed.

Out here was a natural cave, with a couple of tunnels cut through the living rock.

"Well?"

The sound of a gruff voice in the darkness made her jump. She turned to find herself facing a man wearing night-vision goggles. He took them off and switched on a flashlight of his own. In the dim light she could see his wide face, close-cropped brown hair, and the SIG Sauer in his free hand.

"You're alone?"

"Yes."

His name was Phil Martin, and he had been her guide through the maze of underground caves that led to the back door of the bunker. He holstered the gun.

At first, she hadn't liked working with him. He could be brusque and bossy. Sometimes it seemed as though his mind was far away—in some place where it was impossible for her to follow—but she'd quickly found that he knew every aspect of his job, from weaponry to spelunking to psychological motivation. To be honest, she knew she never would have gotten this far without his help.

He'd wanted to come with her into the bunker. Because sending in two people increased the risk, she'd done it alone— and made it back.

Still, she knew she was in for an interrogation. As he led her along the corridor, she was glad of the chance to collect her thoughts. She was sure he'd want to look at her face when he asked her questions, so he escorted her down the tunnel to a place where she could see warm, artificial light shining. It was coming from inside a twelve-by-twelve-foot room that had been carved out of the rock. At the back was a side tunnel that led to a smaller room used for sanitary facilities.

As soon as they stepped inside their living space, Martin

turned toward her, the way she'd known he would, and she saw that his skin was flushed.

"Are you okay?" she asked.

He dismissed the question with a brusque jerk of his arm. "I'm fine. Did you make contact with Baker?"

"Yes."

"How is he?"

"Confused, like we expected."

"What happened?"

"We talked," she answered, making her voice as matter of fact as possible. They'd done a lot more than hold a conversation, but she wasn't going to get into anything she wouldn't have told her mother.

"Talked about what?"

"Old times. And his current situation."

"But you didn't give anything away."

"I didn't like lying to him. I told him not to spill his guts to Montgomery."

"We don't know how much we can trust him."

"I trust him!"

"They could already have messed with his mind enough to make him report that he talked with you."

"No!" she said automatically.

Ignoring her, Martin went on, "He could have a time bomb ticking inside his head. You don't know what kind of crap they've shoveled into his brain."

She couldn't deny that. When she sighed, Martin picked up on it immediately.

"What?"

"He thinks he's in Thailand. They told him he was part of a diplomatic mission that got caught in a bird-flu epidemic. They have him in the bunker for his own protection."

"Or that's a story he told you."

"I'm sure he believed it."

"Why?"

She kept her gaze steady and her voice even. "First, because that's a lot to make up on the spur of the moment. Second, I'm a trained psychologist. That's why you picked me for this job."

"And because you went to school with Baker."

"Look, you can't have it both ways. Either he's lying to me, or he's saying what they made him believe."

"Unfortunately, you don't know which."

"I volunteered to go on this mission because I want to save him. Don't make my job harder."

Something she couldn't quite read flashed in his eyes. "Believe me, I'm not trying to add to your problems. I'm trying to make sure you get out of this alive."

"Don't you want to come out of this alive?" she snapped.

"What do you think?" he answered.

She stared at him for another moment, then turned to one of the cots along the wall and sat down. She'd told him she could tell when someone was lying to her. She wished that applied to Phil Martin. He was hiding something. She knew that much, and she hoped it wasn't something that would sink the mission.

She stretched out her legs, rotating her ankles in their low-rise hiking boots. She would have lain down and slung her arm over her eyes, but she didn't, because she knew Phil was watching her carefully.

"When I said he was in danger, he asked to come with me. That was a logical response on his part."

"What did you tell him?" Martin asked immediately.

"That his leg isn't strong enough."

"What about his leg?"

"He was shot. He thinks that happened in Thailand."

"Good answer on your part." He waited a beat, then asked, "Can he make the trip out of here?"

"I think so."

"But you don't know."

"He won't be worse off than he is now."

"True," Martin conceded.

"I need to relax. Twice I was almost caught." She didn't explain how she'd hidden in Jonah's bed with him lying on top of her.

"Yeah. Try to get some sleep. I'm going to see if I can contact home base."

"Okay."

He turned down the light to a soft glow, then stepped out into the corridor. She heard him trying to use the special radio that he'd been given, but it was obvious that they were too far underground, and the tons of rock above them were preventing him from getting through.

So they were on their own.

He'd looked sick when he'd gone out. Sick or in pain. But moments later when he came back, he appeared to be in better shape.

Was he on drugs? His behavior was consistent with an addict. He'd seem sick and shaky, then he'd disappear and come back looking a lot better.

Did that mean he'd fooled everyone else involved in this assignment—and she was the only one who had picked up on the secretive behavior?

That certainly left her in a precarious situation.

He came back in and leaned against the wall for long moments, staring at her as though he had similar doubts about her.

Finally he turned down the lights farther, then lay down on the other cot. Mercifully, he didn't ask any more questions about her encounter with Jonah.

She was left alone with her own thoughts.

She wished that Martin would turn the light all the way off. She didn't want him to see how shaken she was. On the other hand, that would leave them in total darkness, and she didn't like that alternative either.

She wanted to fold her arms across her chest and hug herself. Instead, she pulled the covers up to her chin, which made sense in the chilly air of the cave. To give herself the illusion of privacy, she closed her eyes.

As she'd matured, she'd come to the conclusion that there was no point in lying to herself. Truth be told, she'd been in love with Jonah Baker all those years ago. A very stupid move, since he apparently wasn't planning to return any deep emotions.

But that one night with him had been the most wonderful experience of her life. Even at twenty-one, he was a fantastic lover. From her previous—and very scant—experiences, she'd thought that sex must be overrated. He'd proved that she didn't have a clue about how good it could be.

Behind her closed lids, she found herself reliving the memories of that night—reinforced by the very recent memories in his bedroom. Every touch. Every kiss. Every whispered word.

Those brief, intimate moments with him in his room proved that nothing had changed inside her head. Jonah Baker was still the man who did it for her.

Sliding her hands to the side of the cot, she gripped the aluminum frame, willing herself to calm down.

Maybe if she focused on the bad stuff, she could regain her cool.

Like what he was going to say when she told him she'd gotten married in an effort to forget him, then given up and gotten divorced two years later because she'd finally admitted she'd married the wrong man.

For an unwelcome moment, George's face floated into her

mind. She hadn't done him any favors by walking down the aisle with him. She hadn't known it at the time, but she'd been using him. Of course, she'd figured out that he'd been using her, too.

But maybe she wouldn't even have to tell Jonah about her mistake of a marriage. Maybe it wasn't going to be an issue at all because nothing would really change. He wouldn't tell her why he hadn't called, and she wouldn't tell him how devastated she had been. After this, they could go their separate ways again, and she'd return to searching for a man who could substitute for him—even when she knew the quest was doomed to failure.

She clenched her teeth, struggling not to make any noise and give anything away to the man lying in the next cot. She could hear him breathing. It wasn't a pleasant sound.

She didn't much like Phil Martin. But she was a realist. She was stuck working with him. If she wanted to help Jonah, she was going to have to rely on Phil's judgment.

When Phil had first come to her office at Howard County Mental Health with the information that Jonah Baker was in danger, she hadn't believed him. The documents he'd brought along served as proof she couldn't ignore, and once she understood what was at stake, she'd had no choice but to go along with the scenario Phil had outlined.

She wanted to save Jonah. She wanted an excuse to be with him again.

Of course, she'd come to realize that Phil had thought someone working in a low-paying government job couldn't pull her weight on the mission. She'd found out later that some of the others on the team had informed him she didn't need the income, and she'd picked the job because she saw it as an opportunity to help people who'd gotten shafted by "the system."

After that, he'd settled down and gotten to work. And the team had given her a lot of information about Jonah. She'd eagerly lapped it up because it filled in so many of the blank spaces that had kept her wondering over the years.

He'd had ranger training at Fort Benning. After that, he'd been on some hair-raising missions—every one of them successful. He was good at his job. He'd served with distinction and he'd earned a Distinguished Service Cross, no small achievement.

Then he'd gotten sent to a village in Afghanistan, on an assignment that had obviously had a hidden agenda. Only she didn't know what it was. And neither did Phil Martin.

When nobody on Jonah's team had reported back, he had been declared missing in action, presumed dead. Only it turned out that he was alive and at the mercy of a bastard named Carlton Montgomery.

And now he needed her help.

She shuddered.

Martin and his group had made her go through a week of intensive training. She'd thought she was prepared, but now she knew she was in over her head.

Because the training exercises had been just that—exercises carried out in an environment that she knew was safe. Or maybe she'd felt comfortable because she hadn't been able to cope with the enormity of what she had to do.

But everything had changed. Once she'd stepped inside the bunker, reality had slammed into her like a speeding train.

JONAH LAY AWAKE for what seemed like hours, staring into the darkness.

He still didn't remember enough about his personal life to fill a two-hour made-for-TV movie. But he was pretty sure he'd never been married. He had the feeling that his memories of Sophia had kept him from hooking up with anyone else.

He blinked in the darkness. If that were really true, why hadn't he tried to make something work out with Sophia?

Because he'd been too young and too stupid to realize what he was throwing away. Or maybe he'd been afraid that one night was enough for her. A novelty. She'd made love with him because it fulfilled one of her own fantasies—connecting with the big bad boy of Centennial High on a very intimate level.

Tonight, though, it had seemed as if she cared. They'd touched each other, and they'd been right back where they were ten years ago. Or that was the way it had seemed to him.

He sighed in the darkness. The longer he lay here, the more he second-guessed their encounter. And second-guessing her wasn't doing him any good. Gritting his teeth, he switched to another topic—his work.

He was more certain about that. At least Sophia had triggered his memories. Bits and pieces of his military career were coming back to him.

The enemy weapons ship he and a crack team had blown up in the Persian Gulf. The helicopter mission to raid a desert stronghold in Iran. The operation to rescue an army team captured by Shiite militia. Expeditions into the territory along the Pakistani border where you could get shot by troops from either Pakistan or Afghanistan.

As far as he knew, he'd been good at his job—until that village that shimmered in his dreams.

If he'd ever really been there. Clenching his fists, he struggled to relax when he wanted to get up and pace around the room.

He stayed where he was, because pacing wouldn't do the leg any good. Besides, he needed to get some sleep.

Finally he fell into a restless slumber. Soon after that, he was back in the heat and dust of Afghanistan.

The sun beat down on him as he pressed against the wall of a house that looked as though it had stood in that place for three hundred years. Again he heard the gunfire in the brown hills. This time the members of the team had split up and he was sneaking around, trying to get in back of Lieutenant Calley so he could shoot him.

He woke, covered with sweat. Swinging his legs over the side of the bed, he cradled his head in his hands, wondering if he'd ever fragged an American officer.

He was still sitting up when he heard a knock at his door.

His heart leaped. Sophia!

But when the door opened, he saw a man wearing the same blue uniform and cap that she had worn the night before.

Jonah squinted at the black name tag the guy was wearing. Sergeant Lopez. That was the only indication of the guy's rank.

Did Jonah's own shirts have a name and rank?

He hadn't even thought to look.

"You're up. Good. Breakfast at 0630. Get a move on."

He tipped his head to the side, looking at the man. "You come around and wake everyone up?"


SOPHIA AWOKE with a start. Jonah was up. And he was talking to someone. And more important, the bug she had planted under the slat at the side of the bed was working. She hadn't really had much faith in the small device, but apparently the men who had designed it knew what they were doing.

There was still a problem. Would someone find it?

She glanced to her right and saw that Martin's bed was empty. Glad of the privacy, she listened to the conversation.

Jonah had just asked the other speaker if he came around to wake everyone up. And the guy answered in the negative.

"Why me?" Jonah asked.

Several seconds passed before the man answered. "Your alarm clock was broken. I said I'd wake you."

"Thanks," Jonah said. Then asked, "This place doesn't have a public address system?"

"No. It was built in the fifties."

"Yeah. Okay," he answered, thinking that even his high school had had a public address system. It wasn't exactly advanced technology.

"I have your morning pill."

Sophia went rigid. This guy had come to give Jonah his medication. That was the real reason he was there.

"Uh, thanks."

There was a long pause, and Sophia waited with her heart pounding.

"Let me get you some water."

"Thanks," Jonah said again.

Seconds stretched, and she strained to hear what was going on. Had he taken the pill?

There was no more conversation on the other end of the line. Several seconds passed before the door closed again. The transmitter was so sensitive that Sophia heard Jonah let out a sigh. Then the bed creaked as he got up.

"Did you take the pill?" she demanded, knowing he couldn't hear her.

Of course he didn't answer.

She strained her ears and heard him make a small sound of pain, probably when he put weight on the injured leg. She'd used the injury as an excuse for not taking him out of the bunker right away. Now, though, she wondered how much of a problem it really would be.

Footsteps crossed the room, then another door shut, and she thought he must be in the bathroom.

So now what?

Either he'd taken the pill, or he'd convinced the guard that he'd taken it. Then he'd be going out into the general population of the bunker, and she was sure that meant everything she'd worked to make him believe would come into question.

JONAH WALKED to the bathroom and closed the door behind him. After using the toilet, he peered at his face in the mirror and rubbed his fingers over the stubble. He looked like a man who hadn't gotten much sleep. That might actually be his normal state, if nightmares kept waking him up any time he drifted off.

As he showered, he thought about the night before. Had Sophia really been there? Or had he summoned her from his imagination because he needed something positive in his life? Something that didn't involve this bunker.

Turning off the water, he reached for a towel, thinking that if he was desperate to wrap himself in fantasies of Sophia Rhodes, maybe he was cracking up.

Back in the bedroom, he pulled on a T-shirt and briefs and did a few stretching exercises, noting how his wounded arm and leg reacted. They were stiff, but better than the night before, he thought.

So was he getting physical therapy in this place?

He took down a uniform shirt and found that it did indeed have a name tag. Major Baker.

Not the usual kind of military insignia. But this wasn't the usual kind of military facility, either.

He noted that he didn't have a cap. Maybe only the enlisted men wore them.

After dressing, he inspected himself in the bathroom mirror. Then he crossed the room to the bed, intending to make it. Instead, he picked up the edge of the sheet and brought it to his nose.

He thought he detected the faint scent of Sophia's skin, and his body reacted instantly.

He made a strangled sound. All he had to do was think he smelled her to get hard.

Did the scent mean she'd really been here? Or perhaps he was just kidding himself, inventing the sensory input along with the encounter.

He went back to making the bed, trying to wipe away the evidence of his tossing and turning the night before—or of anything else that had taken place in the bed.

After exiting the room, he stood for a moment looking up and down the corridor. Did he know where to find the mess hall? If he'd been here for three weeks, he must have been there many times. So he turned right and let his feet carry him along, striving not to limp.

When he reached a cross corridor, he turned right. Then left down another hallway.

The sound of forks clacking against china and men talking drifted toward him. Apparently he was walking in the right direction.

He found the mess hall, where ten uniformed men were sitting at tables eating breakfast. They all looked tough and capable. More than tough, actually. Many had the hard edge of guys destined to get kicked out of the service.

Some glanced at him, while others kept their eyes trained on their plates. He felt like the center of attention. But maybe that was paranoia again.

A stainless-steel counter was fixed to one wall of the room. On it were several large, rectangular stainless serving dishes. Crossing to them, he found scrambled eggs, bacon, toast, butter, jam and oatmeal. A large urn held coffee.

As he served himself, a question popped into his mind.

Turning, he addressed the man closest to him, his face a study in guilelessness.

"So how do they get eggs when they've got a bird-flu epidemic?"

## Chapter Five

Jonah heard somebody across the room cough.

Then a man whose name tag read Colonel Edwards, who looked to be in his fifties, with a lined face but a trim body, answered, "Freeze-dried."

"Oh. I hope we don't run out," Jonah answered.

One of the enlisted men laughed. "Yeah."

"We're well supplied," Colonel Edwards advised.

Jonah stood with his tray, looking around, feeling like a character who had stepped into a play without knowing his lines.

One of the men noticed him standing there and motioned him over. "There's a seat over here."

"Thanks."

He sat down across from two lieutenants, Faraday and Olson, and took a bite of eggs. They didn't taste freeze-dried, but he wasn't going to challenge the colonel.

"How you doin'?" Faraday asked, like they knew each other and had talked yesterday.

"Okay." He took a bite of bacon, wondering how much he would give away by asking questions. Finally he cleared his throat. "Is there any way to get news from outside?"

"I'm afraid we're restricted here," Olson said. "The communications equipment was old and broken."

Jonah considered that inconvenient turn of events. "Then how will we know when it's safe to come out?"

"I assume they'll come and get us," Faraday said.

"Yeah," Olson chimed in, then looked at his watch. "I've got to leave soon. I have an appointment with Montgomery."

Jonah shifted in his seat. "How come?"

"I've got some trouble coping with the stress of getting into this place."

"You mean you didn't like shooting those civilians who were trying to keep us from escaping?" Faraday asked.

"Not much."

Jonah nodded. He didn't like it, either. If it was true. Before he'd walked in, he'd been ready to believe Sophia's story—that nefarious forces were holding him captive in an underground bunker.

Now he wasn't as sure.

"Are you on medication?" he asked Olson.

The man looked startled. His gaze darted across the room. When nobody came to his aid, he cleared his throat. "I don't like to talk about that," he muttered.

"Yeah," Jonah agreed. He could understand that.

Apparently, he wasn't the only guy under stress because of the circumstances. Or was this all a setup?

Under the table, he clenched his fist, wishing he knew which way to jump.

DR. CARLTON MONTGOMERY muttered an oath under his breath. Calling on his self-discipline, he gave himself thirty seconds to deal with his anger, then rearranged his features and pressed one of the buttons on his phone. Moments later, Lieutenant Tobias knocked on the door.

"Come in."

The lieutenant stood across the desk, waiting for instructions.

"I was looking at the security tapes from last night," Montgomery began. "There's a gap of several hours."

"I'm sorry, sir."

"How did it happen?"

"It must have been a malfunction."

Montgomery kept his voice even. "Were there any reports of out-of-the-ordinary incidents? Any personnel who were some place they weren't supposed to be?"

"I'll check the log."

"Do that." He forced himself not to drum his fingers on the desk.

"I want to see Baker. As soon as he's finished breakfast, tell him he has an appointment with me."

Tobias shifted his weight from one foot to the other.

"Yes?" Montgomery asked, unable to keep an undercurrent of annoyance out of his voice.

"Um—we discussed having one of the men in the cafeteria say he had to leave early for an appointment with you. That way Baker wouldn't think he was the only one."

He remembered that now and struggled for calm. A lot was riding on this assignment, and he didn't intend to blow it because he was being pressured to produce.

"Send him to physical therapy after breakfast. Then have him come here." He looked at his watch. "In an hour and fifteen minutes."

"Yes, sir."

Tobias left, and Montgomery shuffled through the papers on his desk. He didn't like the camera failure. Then again, that was what you got when your bunker had been built more than forty years ago. Your equipment wasn't state-of-the-art.

He leaned back in his chair, thinking about the upcoming interview. And about security.

No one in this place had a cell phone, and all the desk instruments were internal only. The only outside communications were through the phone on his desk and the computers in this office.

He reached out his hand toward the phone, thinking he might ask for some instructions. Then he pulled his arm back. He'd been the one who wanted to try this experiment. He'd been so sure it would work. Unfortunately Baker's wounds had gotten infected, and he'd been on too much pain medication for any psychiatric sessions. When he'd finally recovered physically, his damn dreams had started, and Carlton was pretty sure the man didn't want to face the truth.

Carlton sighed. If he admitted that he was beginning to doubt the protocol, that would show weakness, and weakness was the last image he wanted to project. No matter what, he had to make it clear he was calm and in control.

JONAH WAS PUSHING around eggs and bacon on his plate when he noticed an officer striding toward him. He sat up straighter and looked inquiringly at the man, whose name tag read Lieutenant Tobias.

"I want to remind you that you have a physical therapy appointment scheduled in twenty minutes. Then you're scheduled to see Colonel Montgomery."

He struggled not to react to the mention of Montgomery—or to the realization that until the present moment he'd had no idea what he was supposed to be doing today.

From the corner of his eye, he could see several of the men in the mess hall watching him. When he made eye contact with one of them, the guy glanced quickly down at his plate.

Now that everyone was listening, Jonah wondered what he should say. Did he want everyone here to know he was having memory lapses? Or did they already know? After all, Olson had said he was going to see Montgomery. So apparently it was no secret.

He settled on a simple, "Thank you."

At least they were making an effort to rehab him.

As he stood, another question occurred to him. He assumed he would wear gym clothes to physical therapy. Were they in his room?

He guessed he'd find out. And maybe his feet would tell him where to find the gym.

He was halfway down the hall when another thought struck him. This was pretty poor planning. Physical therapy right after breakfast? Lucky he hadn't eaten a full meal, because that was a setup for stomach cramps.

He hurried back to his room and shuffled through the chest of drawers—where he did indeed find gym shorts and a T-shirt. And there were tennis shoes and socks in the bottom of the closet.

After he dressed, he lay down on the bed, trying to picture the route to the gym. Feeling a little shaky, he gripped the wooden slats at the sides of the bed and encountered something that shouldn't be there. A flat metal strip attached to the far side of the frame. When he pulled it out and held it up, he felt his stomach knot.

It was a bug. Somebody had put it there to listen to him.

But who?

The encounter of the night before came zinging back to him. He and Sophia had had plenty to say to each other. Stuff that could get him into trouble. So far, nobody had reacted to the conversation, or come to arrest him, for that matter.

Was Montgomery going to say something or somehow use the information?

He carefully put the thing back where he'd found it, wondering if he'd made a lot of static in somebody's ear by handling it.

A small detail from the night before came back to him. Sophia had banged her knuckles against the wall.

Had she been planting the listening device? Was she the one checking up on him? Better her than somebody else?

He glanced toward the side of the bed. "So, did you plant the bug I just found?" he asked, grinning as he pictured her startled expression when she heard the direct question. Too bad he wouldn't get an answer.

He thought about the pill Lopez had brought him this morning. He'd pretended to take it. Then, when the sergeant had left, he'd flushed it down the toilet.

He'd like to tell that to Sophia since she'd warned him not to swallow the medication. He couldn't take the chance, though, in case he was wrong about how the bug had gotten here. He hadn't given her away. If someone else was listening, they'd think he was addressing *them.* Wondering if he'd made a mistake by talking out loud, he moved restlessly on the bed.

Damn! He was starting to feel as jumpy as a tomcat staring down a Doberman.

Maybe he'd made another mistake not taking the medication. Maybe it would have calmed him down.

Or would it muzzy his brain again?

Instead of getting up, he folded his arms across his chest and lay with his eyes closed for a few minutes, ordering himself to chill.

When he thought he was going to be late if he waited any longer, he got out of bed and started down the hall again—in the direction of the mess hall. Only he kept going and did indeed come to a gym. So, even if he thought he couldn't remember squat about this place, his feet seemed to have some kind of knowledge of their own.

The facility was empty except for one guy wearing gym clothes. Again Jonah was grateful for the name tags.

"How are you doing?" Sergeant Henry asked.

"Better."

The sergeant got out a folder and consulted a chart. "You've regained eighty percent function in the arm and seventy-five in the leg," he said.

"Yeah."

"Why don't you warm up with ten minutes on the bike? Then we'll do your exercises."

He climbed on the recumbent bike, set it to level four and started pedaling. The rhythm was soothing, and he focused on the physical activity.

"So, are you still having those dreams about Afghanistan?" Henry said in a conversational tone.

"I told you about them?" he asked before he could evaluate whether the question was a good idea.

"Well, you were on edge, so I asked you what was wrong, and you talked about it some."

Jonah nodded.

"You want to talk some more?"

"No."

"Sure."

When his ten minutes were up, Jonah climbed off the bike and got down on a mat, where he worked with a big blue ball for a while then went on to stretches.

They finished in time for him to rush back to his room, take another quick shower, then dress in his blue uniform.

He should be planning what to say to Montgomery.

But had he ever planned his conversation before? Would he come across as canned if he tried?

The hole in his memory made him want to scream, but he kept his face impassive as he strode down the corridor again. He let himself walk to the mess hall, then turn in the other direction from the gym.

The corridor ended at a closed door, which was solid at the bottom with glass at the top.

Beyond it he could see a small, square room and the Lieutenant named Tobias sitting at a desk. The man looked up, saw him and motioned him inside.

"Just a moment," he said.

On a sudden impulse, Jonah looked around and asked, "Olson's finished?"

Tobias blinked as though he didn't know what Jonah was talking about. After several long seconds, he nodded. "Yes."

Jonah half turned. It sounded like Olson hadn't been here at all. Or was he only looking for clues to bolster Sophia's side of the case?

He could have taken one of the chairs along the wall. Instead, he stood while the man lifted a phone receiver and dialed a number.

After listening to someone on the other end of the line, he said, "You can go right in." When he gestured toward a door in back of him, Jonah strode to it and turned the knob.

He stepped into a room that was a lot more homey than the rest of the installation. Someone had covered the cinder-block walls with drywall painted a warm apricot. Berber carpeting covered the tile floor. In addition to the desk at one side of the room there were two comfortable easy chairs grouped on either side of a lamp table.

It was a scene out of a fifties movie, except for the berber. That was more recent.

The man behind the desk was tall and slender, with slightly stooped shoulders, thinning salt-and-pepper hair and watery gray eyes.

It was the image that had come to Jonah the night before after he'd awakened from the dream. The doctor would have looked at home in a tweed sports coat with leather patches at the elbows, but he was wearing the same blue uniform as everyone else. His, though, had no name tag.

The man was fussing with a briar pipe, lighting it with a match and drawing on the tobacco, which had an aromatic tang.

As soon as Jonah smelled the aroma, he remembered it and remembered that the doctor smoked, which was not allowed in any other part of the bunker. But he supposed rank had its privileges.

What rank was the doctor, anyway?

Jonah was probably supposed to know, so he couldn't ask.

The doctor gave him a warm smile. "How are you doing?"

"Better."

"Good." Montgomery gestured toward one of the easy chairs. "Sit down."

Jonah lowered himself into the chair. He knew this whole setup was designed to help him relax, but he could feel his heart wildly pounding inside his chest.

The doctor took his pipe from his mouth, came around the desk and sat down in the other easy chair. When he was settled, he took another puff.

"How's your memory?" he asked.

"It's still spotty."

"That's one of the symptoms. The medication you've been taking should help with that."

Would it? Or was the truth just the opposite?

"How are you spending your days?"

Jonah drew a blank. Basket weaving? Volleyball? He shrugged.

"The food here is pretty good, considering," the doctor said.

"Yes."

"You went to physical therapy this morning?"

"Yes."

"How was that?"

"Fine." Jonah wanted to scream at him to stop making nice and get on with the real purpose of this little chat, but he managed to sit with his hands resting easily on the chair arms.

"Any more of those dreams about Afghanistan?" Montgomery asked.

In the gym, Henry had asked him the same question. Why were they so important to everyone? What the hell should he answer? If he said no, the colonel could get the truth out of the physical therapist.

Somehow Jonah had the feeling he was damned if he said yes and damned if he said no.

SOPHIA SAT in front of the monitor.

"Where is he?" Martin asked. He'd been out in the cave, and now he was back, looking winded.

"In Montgomery's office."

"Where else has he been this morning?"

"The mess hall. Then he went back to his room and stayed there for over an hour."

She didn't tell Martin that Jonah had apparently found the bug and spoken to her. He'd jump on her for putting it where Jonah could discover it, and it would no doubt show him she had been indiscreet.

"Did he stay in his room?" Martin was saying. "He could have changed his shoes and you wouldn't know he was somewhere else."

"Why would he do that?"

Martin shrugged.

She looked up at him. "Where were you all morning?"

"I went out closer to the cave mouth to make a report and get some instruction. But I still couldn't get through."

"Too bad."

When he didn't volunteer any more information, she turned back to the screen.

She wanted to scream at Jonah that Montgomery's office was

the most dangerous place in the bunker for him. She wanted to tell him to make some excuse and get out of there. But that wouldn't do any good. He didn't have any way of hearing her, except through some kind of psychic bond, and she wasn't putting any faith in that.

Still, she couldn't keep from sending him a silent message. *Don't talk about Afghanistan. Just don't do it. Please. Please believe me that it's important.*

## Chapter Six

Jonah wanted to shift in his seat, but he managed to stay still as a rock.

"I did dream about Afghanistan last night," he said, his tone measured as he watched the doctor's expression turn eager.

Leading the man on a little more, he said, "There were brown hills. I could hear gunfire in the distance."

He stopped, pretending to remember.

Now it was the doctor who shifted in his seat.

Jonah let the silence stretch, waiting him out. Finally Montgomery spoke. "And then what?"

"Then Lieutenant Calley came striding into the village."

The doctor blinked. "Who?"

"You know—that guy who was court-martialed for murdering civilians in Vietnam."

"Oh. Right."

Jonah floated a hypothesis. "So the dream couldn't be about anything that really happened?"

The doctor shook his head. "It could—if you're using him as a metaphor for reality."

Jonah stroked his chin, struggling to keep his face sober as he plotted his next move. "I don't remember what Calley looked like in real life. In the dream, he was in his mid-twenties, clean shaven, blue eyes. And his teeth were very white and even. He had on a non-standard uniform. Maybe what they wore back in the sixties. But I can't be sure."

"What he looked like isn't all that important," Montgomery snapped.

"You're sure? Okay."

"Go on."

Still making it up, Jonah continued. "Well, what happened in the dream was that Calley had a big bag slung over his shoulder."

The doctor sat forward. "And?"

So Montgomery was interested in the bag. Why?

"And he started pulling out stuff. At first it was toys and candy and things for the kids. Fun stuff. But then he got serious. He had food rations—powdered milk, big bags of rice and meat in neat plastic-wrapped packages like they came from the grocery store back home."

He stopped short when he noticed Montgomery eyeing him with mistrust.

"You're saying he came to help the people?"

"Yeah. And make their lives more comfortable."

"Okay. What else?"

Jonah had been enjoying himself, and he could have manufactured some more of the tall tale, but he wanted to make another point.

"That's it. I had the feeling something else was going to happen, but before it could, someone woke me up."

"Who?"

"A guard came down the hall, opened my door and shone his light inside. I couldn't see his name tag, so I don't know who it was. Do they do that on a regular basis? It disrupts a guy's sleep."

Montgomery scowled. "I don't know the guard protocols."

*Yeah, sure,* Jonah thought, but he kept the observation to himself.

"But I'll make sure they don't disturb you again."

That was something, anyway. Next time Sophia came to his room, he wouldn't have to worry about a guy with a flashlight barging in.

Montgomery gave his a piercing look. "What are you thinking about now?"

"Why?"

"You have a strange expression on your face."

"I was thinking about an old girlfriend."

"Why?"

Jonah scrambled for an answer and came up with a plausible memory. "Well, we were talking about my room. About the guard opening the door. And I was thinking about a time when I was at Hanna's house. In her bedroom. We were…" He stopped as though thinking about how to phrase his next words. "Her parents were supposed to be out for the evening, and we were half-naked in her bed. When we heard her dad coming up the stairs, I had to duck into the closet. Then, when the coast was clear, I climbed out the window. I loosened the drainpipe on the way down."

The story wasn't made up. It had really happened, but he'd just pulled the girl's name out of the air.

The doctor was still watching him closely. "I thought you were having memory problems."

"Yeah. But your question *triggered* a memory."

"Maybe we can dig up some more memories," Montgomery shot back.

"How?"

"Perhaps hypnosis would be more effective than a dream."

Jonah felt the hairs on the back of his neck prickle. "I don't want to do that."

"Why not?"

"It doesn't feel…comfortable."

The doctor's expression grew brittle. "By not cooperating, you're jeopardizing the safety of everybody in this installation."

Jonah's throat tightened, but he managed to ask, "How?"

"We need information from you."

Wondering if he would get an accurate answer, he said, "Probably you told me before, but I can't remember. What is my diagnosis?"

"You're suffering post-traumatic stress connected with your assignment in Afghanistan. You were in a military hospital for several months after villagers turned you over to American troops."

Jonah considered the implications. He could have asked exactly what was supposed to have happened to him. But he didn't want to hear the doctor's story. If it was a story.

Instead, he asked, "And my next assignment was Thailand?"

"Yes."

"So I was cleared for duty."

"It was supposed to be an easy assignment. The bird-flu epidemic changed everything. You went berserk and endangered the lives of everyone with the diplomatic mission."

Jonah gripped the arms of the chair to steady himself. He had almost gotten a bunch of people killed?

He didn't want to believe it. He didn't want to believe anything this man had told him.

But what if it was true?

Montgomery was looking at him with satisfaction. "Are you sure you don't want to try hypnosis?" he asked, his voice gentle yet persuasive.

Despite his sudden feeling of horror, Jonah answered, "No." If he knew anything, he knew he didn't want this man having that kind of access to his mind. He didn't need Sophia Rhodes to tell him that.

He stared into space, not seeing anything around him. Then,

as if he'd discovered a gateway to freedom, his eyes focused on the clock in the bookcase to his right.

"We're over time," he said, his voice low and gritty.

Montgomery glanced at his watch. "Yes, but I don't have anyone after you. We could keep talking if you want."

"No. This session was…traumatic."

"I understand," Montgomery said, his tone grudging. Getting up, he consulted an appointment book. "We can start again at the same time tomorrow."

"Yes," Jonah answered because he was sure that appearing to cooperate was his only option.

He climbed out of his chair and headed for the door without looking back at the man he knew was watching his every move. The way he walked. The way he held his shoulders.

He'd started off the session feeling like he was in control. By the end he'd felt like he was sliding down a greased slope toward some region of hell. He'd hit the bottom and bounced, and now he was so numb he could barely string two thoughts together in his mind.

Stepping into the waiting room, he closed the door behind him, trying to collect himself. He had to think. He sensed danger from the doctor. He focused on that, trying to build some kind of case for his own sanity when he knew he was hanging on by his fingernails.

At first, Montgomery had given him no hard facts. Then he'd come out with some horrific statements about Major Jonah Baker. But the man's attitude had never changed. It was obvious he wanted information, which seemed to confirm what Sophia had told him.

Sophia. She had come to him in the night and started his mind working again. Well, her and not taking the pills. Before that he had barely been functioning. Had he given that away to Montgomery? He hoped to hell he hadn't.

As though coming out of a fog, he noticed that the waiting

room was empty. The lieutenant who served as a receptionist was gone. Well, he thought, maybe that presented an opportunity….

Montgomery was still in his office with the door closed. Hoping he'd stay there, Jonah crossed to the desk and looked at the computer. A screen saver was showing, indicating that Tobias had been away for a few minutes.

When Jonah tapped one of the keys, he saw a list of men and their duty assignments.

He skimmed it and found only routine stuff—until he came to a notation about checking on Baker.

Apparently several men were assigned to look in on him during the night. Was that really going to change now?

When he found nothing else of interest, he switched to the other window and found himself looking at a pornographic Web site.

So that's what the receptionist had really been doing. But he'd put up the duty list in case anybody saw.

Nice.

As he switched back to the previous screen, another interesting observation zinged into his brain. Olson had told him that they were cut off from the outside world. So how was this computer connected to the Internet?

Jonah's hand twitched. Before he could stop himself he moved the cursor to the taskbar and clicked the Internet button. Several sites seemed to be open. He flicked to another one and found he was looking at a news parody site.

So the bunker wasn't sealed off from communication.

Quickly he restored the screen to its original.

Taking more of a chance, he began quietly opening drawers. In each, he saw only the usual office supplies, until he opened the bottom right-hand drawer and found a metal box. In it, was a stack of ten-, twenty- and fifty-dollar bills.

Struggling to repress a grin, Jonah helped himself to a quarter of the stack, then closed the drawer. Knowing he'd be pressing his luck to stay any longer, he stepped into the hall.

His heart was pounding now, and he forced himself to walk casually—not to his room, the mess hall or the gym, or anywhere else he could remember.

Words and phrases from the conversation with the doctor were swirling in his head again.

*Went berserk.*

*Endangered the mission.*

*Post-traumatic stress.*

He fought to keep his hands at his sides and not press them over his eyes.

Was he really all screwed up? He didn't want to believe it. He couldn't believe it and retain his self-image.

Yet he'd just stolen some money. As a teenager he might have done it, but he didn't think it was the kind of thing the adult Jonah Baker did.

Still, these were extraordinary circumstances. If he got out of here, he was going to need the money. American money. He suspected he would have no problem spending it in Thailand.

He kept walking, knowing he needed something constructive to do instead of thinking what Montgomery had told him. Since he had no idea what this facility looked like, he decided to do some exploring. Would somebody stop him or follow him? He'd soon find out.

SOPHIA'S GAZE was glued to the screen. "He's left Montgomery's office."

"Let's hope he's walking under his own power."

She glanced at Phil. "What do you mean?"

"They could have drugged him. They could be carrying him somewhere."

"No!"

Phil came over and looked at the screen. "Then what's he doing?"

"I don't know."

"Montgomery may be getting desperate."

She dragged in a breath and let it out. "Let's see where Jonah is going."

"Okay," he agreed.

She felt him standing behind her, watching the action like a guy glued to a televised sports event. She wished she had gotten to work with some of the other men who had been in on the briefing sessions, but Phil had volunteered for the assignment, and she was stuck with him.

"Have you been on a rescue mission like this before?" she asked, partly because she couldn't stand the silence.

"No."

Not the answer she wanted to hear. But she felt as if her choices had been taken away when she'd signed up.

"If he gets into a good position, I can pull him out now."

"Not you. Me."

Her head jerked up. "What do you mean? I'm his contact."

"But you could get caught."

"So could you. And he may not trust you."

"He may not trust you, either. You don't know what Montgomery said to him. Or what he said to the doctor. He could have spilled the beans about you."

Containing a spurt of annoyance, she said, "Let's see where he ends up." Instead of looking at Phil, she kept her eyes on the screen.

He shrugged and went to the back of the room, and she saw him taking a drink of water. Was he swallowing a pill? she wondered. She thought she'd seen his hand slide out of his pocket a second before.

This could be further evidence of drug addiction, she thought. Or he could simply be taking stimulants to stay awake.

When he turned a corner, she knew he was heading for the portable toilet. Because there was no door on the facility, they tried to give each other privacy.

She was glad he'd gone there now. At least she'd have a few minutes when he wasn't hanging over her shoulder.

She turned back to the screen, seeing a moving blip that represented Jonah.

In her mind she spoke to him. *Jonah, come on. Come closer to the exit and we can get you out of there.*

CARLTON MONTGOMERY repressed the impulse to smack his fist against the apricot-covered wall.

Instead, he took several deep breaths, then sat down at his desk and opened his laptop computer. In his file on Baker, he wrote down a summary of their session. At first he'd thought he was going to get something from the man this time. Instead, the information was useless.

Was Baker reporting his dream accurately? Or was he working some kind of con?

He wouldn't have considered that possible a few days ago, but the man had seemed different today. More alert and more sure of himself—at least until Carlton had started feeding him the story about his going berserk. That had shaken him up. But he'd still declined the offer of hypnosis.

Montgomery pondered that logic. Baker was being given powerful medication every morning and evening. Had he skipped a dose? Had the sergeants failed to give it to him? Or was he only pretending to take the stuff? Was he in a rebellious phase? What?

After consulting his patient notes, he scribbled a note on the pad next to the computer.

"Question the sergeants about Baker's meds. Have them make damn sure he's taking the pills."

He put down the pen and leaned back in his chair. He'd been giving the man a drug that would induce confusion and interfere with his short- and long-term memory. But was that enough? Maybe it was time for something heavy-duty.

Unfortunately, the strategy could blow up in his face. The drug he was thinking about could fry the man's brain. He'd have to be careful. But if that was his only alternative, he'd have to use it.

JONAH WALKED DOWN the hall in the direction of his room and went past it. Resisting the urge to look behind him or to walk more quickly than normal, he kept going as though he knew what he was doing. He stopped at a random door and opened it to what looked like a dormitory with at least thirty bunk beds arranged in rows. All of them had mattresses but no sheets, which must mean nobody was sleeping there.

He wondered if most of the men here slept in dorms and if he was one of the few with a private room. Perhaps just the officers had that privilege.

He shut the door and kept going down the corridor for several dozen yards, then turned down a side hallway to another door with a sign that said Stairway.

He opened the door and stepped into a stairwell where he descended one level.

As he stood looking around, he flexed his leg. It was sore, but not as bad as it had been the night before.

The corridor wasn't much different from the one on the floor above, except that the lighting wasn't quite as bright.

The first door he came to led to a room with three upright tanks about twenty feet tall and twelve feet across. They were labeled Fresh Water. That made sense in a closed facility. But he didn't see a spigot on the side of the tanks.

He stared at the sign. It was in English, with no translation into anything that looked like Thai.

Well, he'd been told this facility had been constructed by the U.S. government.

He exited and continued down the hall to the next door, which opened into a storeroom lined with shelves of cans of food and boxes of medical supplies, toilet paper and linens. As he walked among the rows of shelves, he noted once again that all the labels were in English, with additional information in Spanish on some of the cans.

It was difficult to believe that they hadn't stocked any indigenous products. It certainly would have been cheaper to buy from the locals than to import everything from the States.

SOPHIA GLANCED over her shoulder. Martin was still in the bathroom, and she wasn't going to go back there for a consultation.

Snatching up the portable GPS locator, she rushed down the corridor toward the hidden door that she'd used to enter the bunker. Jonah was in the storeroom. She knew it. And if she could just get to him in time, she could bring him through. That would solve her biggest problem—how to get him out of there.

"Jonah, stay right where you are," she called out. She knew he couldn't hear her with rock walls between them, but it helped to feel that she was communicating with him.

And he was so close. So close.

Before she could open the door, a hand came down on her shoulder, and she screamed.

JONAH HEARD a muffled scream. Either it was far away—or on the other side of a thick wall. It sounded like a woman, and the only woman he'd seen here was Sophia.

Now it seemed as if she was in trouble, and his heart leaped into his throat, blocking his windpipe.

He wanted to call out to her, but he knew that was the wrong thing to do. Where was she? Had he really heard her?

He moved toward the shelves at the far end of the room, from where he thought the scream had emanated.

As he crossed the room, the door in back of him opened, and a hard voice called, "Hold it right there."

# Chapter Seven

"Don't move," a low voice ordered.

Sophia went stock-still. She knew that the man holding her was Phil Martin. And she knew that he was doing his job—as he saw it.

"What the hell are you up to?" he asked, his voice so low she wouldn't have heard him unless he'd been speaking directly into her ear.

"Jonah's out there."

"And so are a lot of other guys."

She turned toward him. "How do you know?"

"Because I was looking at the seismic indicator. It's very sensitive. And it told me there are eight people about to enter the room on the other side of that door."

She felt her whole body go cold. She ached to open the door and prove Phil wrong, but she knew that was a dumb move. He was the expert at covert operations and she was the rank amateur. So she followed him back the way they'd come.

When she reached their staging area, she looked down at the GPS she'd brought and saw that Jonah was now on the stairs, on his way back to the living area of the bunker.

"They came and got him," Phil said, his voice hard.

"They could hurt him."

"They won't. Not unless they already got what they wanted from him."

It was all she could do to keep from bashing her fists into something. "But we don't know what they've gotten! Why did they come after him just now?"

"Let's be optimistic. Probably they didn't want him messing around down there."

She nodded. That made sense. There was dangerous electrical and mechanical equipment on this floor. Still, she had to ask, "What are we going to do?"

"I'll make a decision and let you know."

FOUR MEN walked in front of Jonah and four in back. Quite a large group to retrieve one lone guy. When the door to the storeroom had opened, he'd been prepared to fight whoever came through the door, but he couldn't handle eight armed men.

The guy in charge of the "rescue squad" had said he could get hurt down in the service area of the bunker. Yeah, sure. Hurt by them. He'd gone along quietly, half expecting them to take him back to Dr. Montgomery for an evaluation of his mental state. Instead they brought him to the mess hall, where lunch was being served.

Why had they come charging after him? Perhaps they were afraid that he'd somehow escape, or at least hide from them. But why did they think he'd do that? Either because he was crazy or because he'd come to his senses.

The speculation brought him back to Sophia. Had he been unconsciously looking for her? And how close had he gotten? She'd sneaked into the bunker *somehow*. It made sense that she'd come through a back exit, not the front door, wherever that was. But why had she screamed? Unless he'd only imagined her startled, frightened cry….

He got a lot of curious and resentful looks when he entered the mess hall. It was obvious these guys considered him a badass. If he'd really put all of their lives in danger, that would certainly generate resentment.

He grabbed a tray, then a plate and helped himself from the buffet on the steam table. He wasn't hungry, but he filled his plate with food and carried it to a table against the wall.

This time, nobody came over to be friendly. Well, what did he expect? He'd just caused them a lot of trouble.

As he took a bite of chicken, he thought again about what was supposed to be going on here. First eggs and now chicken. In the middle of a bird-flu epidemic?

Surely this poultry hadn't come from the countryside, nor did this taste like canned chicken. So was there a henhouse somewhere down in the bunker?

He ate a little bit, then set his tray in the clean-up area and walked down the hall, wondering if he could get back downstairs. But this time, he was thinking more clearly and looked for security cameras. He found them immediately.

He wanted to slap his forehead. That was how they'd known where he was when he'd gone exploring. Which also told him that someone was actively monitoring the security system, so if he strayed from his routine, they'd be right there. His head down so nobody could see his tense expression, he went into a room that served as a recreation area. Some guys were watching an action adventure movie on DVD. Ignoring them, he went to the shelf filled with paperback novels and looked through the collection. All of the books looked well-used. He took a mystery and an adventure novel, which he brought back to his room.

But instead of reading, he pictured the diplomatic mission. The bird-flu scare. The mad rush to safety. And his own failure to keep a cool head.

He made a disgusted sound and picked up the book, forcing himself to scan the pages, even when he wasn't taking in much of the story. Anything was better than thinking about himself.

The exercise got him through to dinner time.

Then he sat in the back of the recreation room for a while, watching another shoot-'em-up movie. Again, he wasn't much interested in the action, but it kept him occupied until ten hundred hours. When he left, he picked up a uniform cap someone had left lying on a table. He jammed it under his arm as he headed for his room like a good boy. But he wasn't planning to stay there long. As soon as the place settled down for the night, he was going to see if he could find Sophia. The hell with the cameras. If he kept his head down, maybe they'd think he was supposed to be in the hallway, patrolling. Of course, he'd heard the scream hours ago. If she was hurt or in danger, maybe he was too late. He hoped to hell not.

But he'd forgotten something important. As he was getting ready to leave the room, a knock on the door startled him. Then Lopez came in.

"Time for your evening medication," he said.

"Yeah. Right." The guy gave him a narrow-eyed look, and Jonah wondered why. Had the sergeant gotten in trouble for not doing his job?

"I watched you take it last time," he muttered.

Jonah nodded.

Lopez brought the pill and a glass of water from the bathroom and handed them to Jonah.

"I DON'T LIKE IT," Phil muttered.

"You've got a better suggestion?" Sophia countered as she tucked her hair under a cap.

"No."

"I go to his room and I get him out of here tonight." She

wanted to shout that they should have done it last night, but there was no use getting mad at Phil. He'd been following the procedure outlined. He'd been instructed to get a report on Jonah's sanity before getting up close and personal.

"I can't keep the cameras off as long as last night."

"It will work out fine." She made herself sound confident although her insides were tied in knots.

This time she was armed—with a gun and the portable GPS. It told her Jonah was in his room.

When she got there, would he trust her enough to leave with her?

As she thought of a half dozen nasty possibilities, she couldn't stop a shiver from racing over her skin. But there was nothing she could do to change anything that had happened now.

Her lips set in a grim line, she turned the handle and opened the door, half expecting someone to spring at her from inside the storeroom. But as far as she could tell, it was empty.

So far, so good. All she had to do now was make contact with Jonah, tell him they were leaving, and hope to God he would come with her.

CONSCIOUS THAT Lopez was watching him like a store security guard tracking a suspected shoplifter, Jonah took the pill. Hoping he looked like a man with nothing to hide, he put the pill in his mouth and managed to get it into the space between his gum and his cheek before swallowing the water.

"Okay," he said, handing back the glass.

But Lopez stayed for more than a minute, watching him. And Jonah had to stand there feeling the pill start to fall apart.

When the guy finally left, Jonah rushed into the bathroom and dug out as much of the thing as he could. Then he rinsed out his mouth, praying that he hadn't swallowed any of the damn stuff by accident.

Heart pounding, he sat down on the edge of the bed, trying to figure out if his brain was getting that muzzy feeling again.

SOPHIA FELT as if razor wire was twisting in her guts. Last night it had seemed that Jonah believed her. But she didn't know what false information Montgomery had fed him during the day. All she knew was that Jonah had figured out she'd bugged him.

She glanced at the screen and saw that he was still in his room. Good!

But just as she'd breathed out a sigh, everything changed.

He stepped into the corridor. He was on the move. Headed for God knew where.

Because she'd thought she was going to meet him in his quarters, she'd plotted a course through the maze of tunnels that made up the bunker. All at once, she was in unknown territory.

She studied the GPS, trying to determine the safest way. She knew the guard schedule along the route she'd intended to take, but she didn't know who might be in the other corridors.

After reading the schematic, she slipped the device into her pocket and hurried along the hallway.

When she came to a cross corridor, she stopped and slid her face just an inch around the corner. Good thing, because a guard was coming toward her.

She hurried back the way she'd come, opened a door, and closed herself into an empty room. With her pulse pounding in her throat, she waited for the footsteps to pass.

It seemed to take forever, but finally she opened the door a crack and found the hallway empty again.

Though she didn't want to waste time, she knew that Jonah could have changed directions while she'd been hiding, so she glanced at the GPS screen again. She was right. This time he was heading toward her. Finally, she'd lucked out.

She kept moving on a collision course with him, so intent on the screen, that she didn't see another guard until he was almost on top of her.

"Hold it right there," he said in a hard voice.

She froze.

Now what? If she ran, she could get shot. And if she stayed where she was, she could end up in Dr. Montgomery's clutches.

"Who the hell are you?"

She didn't answer, only waited for the guard to approach her. When he was close enough to touch, she lashed out a leg, trying to disable him with a kick in the crotch.

He must have been ready for her to try something because he dodged to the side and grabbed her.

As his arm brushed her cap, it fell off, and he made a low exclamation when he saw her blond hair.

"A chick! How the hell did you get in here?"

"Special assignment."

"We'd better ask Dr. Montgomery about that."

"Of course."

She pretended that she had every right to be there. But when he got out a pair of handcuffs, she panicked and flailed out with her arm.

In response, he landed a flat-handed blow on her face that stunned her.

Staggering back, she saw him go for the microphone on his collar. As he reached the button that opened the communications line, a blur of movement made him whip his head to the side. But it was too late. Someone crashed into him, knocking him to the ground and taking Sophia along with him.

Jonah!

When the guard went for his gun, she twisted to the side and bit down on his wrist. He screamed, and slashed toward her face with his spread fingers.

While the man was attacking her, Jonah unsnapped the catch at the top of the man's holster, pulled out his gun and brought the butt down on the guy's head.

He made a gurgling sound and went limp.

"Thanks," Sophia gasped.

"No problem."

Before they could exchange any information, a loud siren blared.

Jonah looked up, his eyes narrowed. "How do we get out of here?"

"Through the storeroom where you were this morning." He helped her up, and she swayed on her feet. Looking wildly around, she expected to see armed men coming at them from both ends of the corridor. But so far it was clear.

"Did I hear you scream?"

She looked at him. "Yes."

"What happened?"

"I couldn't come get you."

"But—"

"We'll talk about it later."

"How did you know I was in there?"

She pulled out the GPS and showed him the blip that indicated where he was. Then she pressed her hand against her forehead, trying to orient herself. "I don't remember how to get there from here," she admitted. "Do you?"

"I hope so."

He didn't have to urge her to hurry. They sprinted down the corridor, then into a cross passage and down a flight of stairs.

Jonah was limping badly by the time they were in sight of the storeroom. Worse, the corridor was suddenly full of uniformed men rushing toward them from both directions.

She opened the storeroom door and flung herself inside. As soon as Jonah was through the door, she turned and locked it, thinking that it wouldn't hold the guards off for long.

"This way."

Behind them, fists pounded on the door. When it didn't open, she heard bullets tearing into the metal.

Jonah swore. "They'll get in. We're trapped."

"Keep going. In back of the shelves."

She led him toward the rear of the room, then behind the shelving where the exit was located.

Behind them, the storeroom door burst open, and guards poured in. "Halt."

Sophia kept running. But one of the pursuers saw Jonah as he followed her behind the shelves.

"Over there."

Guards rushed after him.

"Hurry," Sophia shouted.

Ignoring her, Jonah turned and pushed at the shelves. At first they didn't move. Then they rocked on their base and tumbled forward, hitting several men on the way down and blocking the others.

Jonah turned and dashed after Sophia, through the opening and into the stone tunnel.

WHEN JONAH saw a tough-looking man in a blue uniform waiting on the other side of the door, he reared back. "Who the hell are you?"

"Philip Martin. Better known as the cavalry."

He reached around Jonah, slammed the door, and pulled down an iron bar, sealing off the opening. Then he gestured down a tunnel hewn out of solid rock.

In the dim light, Jonah stared at the man who'd obviously been waiting for Sophia. Who was this guy, really? Could he trust him? Could he trust Sophia, for that matter? Last night she had come to his bedroom with a story about his being held captive. Was she truly trying to rescue him or was Montgomery the one trying to help him? He had no way of knowing what was fiction and what was reality.

"I want some answers," he said in a gritty voice.

"Later," the man named Philip Martin answered.

He grabbed the guy's shoulder. "Don't tell me later! I want answers now. What's your motivation for getting me out of there?"

Phil gave him a hard look. "Special assignment for the DOD."

"What's that supposed to mean?"

"We don't have time for a discussion now."

When Jonah failed to get an answer, he turned to Sophia. "And how did you get involved?"

Before she could speak, loud pounding sounded against the door.

"I think you're going to have to wait for an in-depth discussion," Phil said. "Come on." He turned and hurried down the tunnel.

Sophia cupped her hand over Jonah's shoulder. "We'll talk later."

Not knowing for sure whether they were the good guys, he listened to his gut, then turned and followed Phil.

As they hurried toward a light glowing in the darkness, an enormous blast sounded behind them, the pressure wave throwing them backward down the tunnel.

Jonah grabbed Sophia and curved his body over hers as the floor shook and stones rattled down from the ceiling.

His mind flashed on some of the mine disasters he'd read about in the newspapers. Lord, was the whole tunnel going to come down around them?

He held his breath, praying that the structure was solid. After a few moments, the shaking stopped, leaving them coughing as dust settled around them.

Phil stood and brushed himself off, glancing back the way they'd come.

"It looks like they're through the door."

Jonah still didn't know what was going on. But he knew that armed men would be in the tunnel before the dust cleared.

He gripped Sophia's hand. "Which way?"

Phil pointed toward the light. "There's a room to the left. Stop there and arm yourself. Then keep going. There's a maze of natural caves down there."

Turning, Jonah followed Sophia down the tunnel, toward the lighted area. Beyond his vision was what appeared to be a vast area of blackness.

They stepped into what looked like a campsite. How long had Sophia and Phil been there? he wondered.

He found the gun rack and took two SIG Sauers plus extra clips. While he armed himself, Sophia pulled a pack from under one of the cots and slipped her arms through the straps.

"My emergency supplies," she explained as Phil lifted an Uzi from the rack. She looked at the GPS. "This is broken. I might as well leave it."

They had only taken a few steps toward the blackness beyond the camp when Jonah looked back and realized that Phil wasn't following them.

"What are you doing?"

He gave Jonah a hard look as he pulled out more heavy weaponry. "Getting a surprise ready for them. Go on."

"You—"

"Go on," the other man said again. "I'm going to handle this. You need a head start with that bad leg."

"Okay," he said, conceding the point and assuming Phil would join them quickly.

He and Sophia had covered a hundred yards when someone behind them started shooting. Someone else returning fire.

Phil and the guards.

The exchange went on for several moments, sporadic at first, then with more fury, and he pictured the guards advancing on the lone gunman.

"Come on," he muttered to Sophia. "What are you waiting for?"

The words were barely out of his mouth when the firing suddenly stopped.

## Chapter Eight

Wide-eyed, Sophia looked at him and made a strangled sound in her throat. "Phil…"

He shook his head. "Either they captured him, or they shot him. And I'm not betting he's still alive."

"Lord, no!"

He heard the horror in her voice as the reality slammed into her. It reflected his own feelings. The man was dead—because of him. He would have turned around and charged back, guns blazing, but Sophia grabbed his arm, grounding him.

"You can't go back there."

He might want to even the score—for Phil, a guy he hadn't known very long, and for himself, too—but he'd end up getting himself killed. That wasn't an option because the men who had shot Phil would shoot Sophia, too. After they tortured her to find out who she was and why she was here.

The hell of it was that he didn't even know the answer to that question.

He didn't share any of that thinking with Sophia. Instead he said, "I assume you know the way out of here?"

"Yes."

She breathed out a sigh as he hurried along beside her. In a few minutes, they reached a place where the tunnel opened out into blackness.

"Now what?"

"Give me a minute."

Sophia pulled the pack off her back and fumbled inside. Bringing out two pairs of night-vision goggles, she handed him one.

With no natural light in the cave, it was still almost impossible to see. Then she brought out flashlights that emitted an infrared beam—which illuminated several markings on the wall.

"Bread crumbs," Sophia whispered.

Behind them, he could hear voices. "We've got to hide," he said in a barely audible voice.

"Not to worry. This place is hide-and-seek heaven."

She grabbed his free hand and led him to the left, behind an outcropping of stalagmites, then around another bend so that they were further sheltered from the tunnel. They both switched off their infrared lights.

Almost as soon as they'd ducked into hiding, three guards appeared. All of them were holding flashlights, which they swung in an arc. With the night-vision goggles, the light hurt Jonah's eyes, and he took off the goggles.

"Baker and the woman went down here."

One of them swore. "But this is a big mother of a cave. They could be anywhere."

"We go in there, we could get lost," the third one said. "We'd better go back and get some more lights."

The others agreed.

The lights swivelled in the other direction, but Jonah waited until they had disappeared back into the tunnel. "We have to hustle," he said.

"Right." She stood unmoving beside him, and he wondered

what she was doing, until she reached for him and wrapped her arms around him.

For a moment he was startled. Then he circled her shoulders and pulled her against him. He could feel her trembling.

"Cold?"

"Scared."

"You did fine."

"I didn't know it was going to be this rough." She swallowed hard. "I didn't know Phil was going to get killed."

"Yeah. Let's make sure it wasn't for nothing." He waited a beat, then said, "Maybe this is when you tell me who sent you here."

She hitched in a breath. "An outfit called the Light Street Detective Agency."

"Who are they?"

"They're in Baltimore. They do some government contract work, and they were contracted by a Department of Defense office that wanted to know what Montgomery was up to."

"So the point of the exercise wasn't rescuing me."

He felt her tense. "No. But it was the point for me."

"Okay."

"You don't believe me?"

"I don't know what the hell to believe anymore."

He wanted to ask if she would have backed out if she'd known the guards were out for blood, but he kept that question locked behind his lips.

Last night, she had kissed him passionately. Today she kept her head tipped down. So was she trying to change the terms of the relationship?

If he kissed her again, he might find out. But he couldn't do it now. Not when the guards were coming back.

She held him for long seconds before easing away.

"We'd better go."

They both put on their night-vision goggles and switched on their beams again. She moved hers in a circle and found one of the marks on the floor. Once she had her bearings, she began leading him across the cavern, where they had to keep detouring around stalagmites and ducking under stalactites.

Figuring he had nothing to lose, he began asking questions in a low voice. "How long was I in the bunker?"

"Three weeks."

He muttered a curse under his breath. "And I don't remember any of it—until last night, when you woke me up. Well, I do have a few memories. I could find my way to the mess hall, the gym and Montgomery's office."

"At first your wound was infected. You were on heavy pain meds, so there was no chance of getting information out of you. They had to get you well first."

"How do you know all that?"

"The Light Street people had a lot of information on you."

"Like what?"

"Your service record."

"Some of that information is classified."

"I know. You did some really heroic things. You got the Distinguished Service Cross."

"I did my job," he answered.

"Right. And how many guys get the DSC?"

She changed the subject abruptly. "I need to know—did you take any medication today?"

In the darkness, he could hear her draw in a breath and hold it.

"No. A guy named Lopez came to give it to me, and I only pretended to take it."

"I heard that—over the microphone."

"So you *were* the person who planted it."

"Yes."

"Lopez was more persistent when he came back this evening. I'm thinking he got chewed out."

"Good."

"Yeah." He laughed. "I didn't take it the night before, either. I found the pill under the pillow."

"I guess you had come to the right conclusions. But your logic was still a little fuzzy."

"It's a lot better now."

"I can tell."

Another thought struck him.

"You said the GPS was broken, but show me where you put the transponder."

"Your right shoe." She knelt down and reached under the laces. When she pulled out a small metal disk, he took it away from her and crushed it in his fingers.

As they resumed walking, he kept hitting her with questions so she wouldn't have a chance to prepare her answers.

"How exactly did you get hooked up with the Light Street people? I mean, why did they come to you?"

"I'm a clinical psychologist."

"Convenient. So you're in a great position to evaluate the escapee's mental state."

"That's not why."

"But Phil wouldn't agree to have you bring me out until you gave him a report."

Her breath caught. "How do you know that?"

"It made sense. And you came looking for me tonight. So the leg was just an excuse. It's about the same as the last time you saw me."

After a pause she said, "You asked how I got involved. It's because Kathryn Kelley, another psychologist, is a friend of mine. She's got an office at 43 Light Street and her husband,

Hunter Kelley, works for Randolph Security, which is associated with them. She came to me after they found out you knew me."

He still didn't get all the implications, so he let her continue.

"She told me you were in danger. When she explained what was going on, I couldn't leave you there."

Her voice sounded sincere. He wished he could see her face, but that was impossible in the dark.

Although he kept pushing ahead, the injured thigh was starting to show the strain. Finally he knew that he had to stop for a few minutes.

He cleared his throat. "I hate to slow us down, but I need to rest the leg."

She turned toward him immediately. "I'm so sorry. I should have thought of that."

"Not your problem."

"Of course it is." She made a low sound. "I mean, we're in this together."

Turning, she ran her light over the trail ahead. "Actually, we stopped a little way farther along on the way in. There's a place we can sit."

"So we're about halfway?"

"Yes."

She led him to a flat rock that could serve as a bench.

He eyed the height. "It's better if I sit on the floor and stretch out my leg."

"Sure."

Gingerly, he lowered himself to the ground, and she sat beside him.

Stretching his leg straight out, he massaged the sore muscles. Then, because he wanted to torture himself some more with all the reasons why he and Sophia had nothing in common, he said, "So you went to college after I left."

"Yes. I went to Radcliffe. Then Hopkins for my Master's and Ph.D."

He pictured what her life must have been like. Probably her parents had paid for her to live in an apartment while she was in school. She would have had a car, joined a sorority, gone to parties and football games.

All the while, he'd been crawling through muddy obstacle courses and learning how to kill people. Then relaxing in the evenings with the guys at a local bar or picking up willing women in town.

"What are you thinking?" she asked.

"You know I never furthered my education after high school. And I was lucky to graduate from there."

"Because you didn't apply yourself. After that, you got a lot of life experience in the army."

"That doesn't give us much in common."

"Are you worried about that?" she asked in a soft voice.

He wasn't sure how to answer. A yes implied he was thinking about the future. A no would make him sound arrogant.

"It puts us on an unequal footing," he finally said. Because the night-vision goggles were starting to get uncomfortable, he took them off. Beside him, Sophia did the same.

"I don't see that as a major problem."

Either she was trying to say that they wouldn't be together for very long or that she didn't see their wildly different educations as a barrier between them.

When he remained silent, she asked, "Are you trying to push me away?"

He honestly didn't know. And why would he? Because he didn't trust her, or because he thought she didn't want him, and he was trying to strike first?

While he was mulling that over, a sound seeped into his consciousness. At first he thought the guards might have caught up with them. Then he realized he was hearing a deep rumbling.

He swore sharply.

"What?" she asked, her voice turning anxious.

Without the goggles, he couldn't see into the darkness, but he was pretty sure what was happening.

"Get down!" As the rumbling grew closer, he pushed her to the ground beside him and flung his body over hers.

It was difficult to hear anything besides a roaring noise now, but he pressed his mouth to her ear and said, "Landslide. The explosion must have triggered it."

To their right, where they would have been walking, he felt debris tumbling down a steep slope.

As he had earlier, he shielded her, draping his body over hers. He was aware of her breasts pressing against his chest, her hips sandwiched between his and the ground, one of her legs thrust between his.

He tried to ignore the intimate position as rocks pounded to their right. A few small ones hit him, but he stayed where he was.

She clung to him, her face pressed to his shoulder as the rubble tumbled downward. After long moments, the earth finally stopped shaking.

Once again, dust wafted around them, and he kept her face shielded until the worst of it settled to earth.

Then he raised his head. Unable to see her in the darkness, he asked urgently, "Are you okay?"

"Yes. Are you?"

"Some small stuff hit me."

"You'll have bruises," she said, reaching up to stroke her hands gently across his back.

"I'm not worried about that."

"If you hadn't stopped to rest, we would have been under a pile of rubble now."

"Yeah," he answered in a gritty voice.

"Thank God for that."

The emotion in her voice mirrored what he felt. When she pulled him back down and angled her head so that her lips met his, he was as eager for the contact as she.

He made a rough sound as the reality of their narrow escape hit him. A little while ago, he had been wondering about her motives. Now he felt her clasping him against her breasts.

His lips settled on hers, sealing their mouths together, and he knew by her response that was what she wanted.

His emotions leaped up to meet hers. He had made love to many women since the night they had spent in bed together. A lot of those times had been good. But none as good as it had been with Sophia Rhodes.

He'd known all along that he was comparing other women to her. Nobody else had ever measured up.

Now, though, she was back in his arms and he was lying on top of her.

Holding her to him, he rolled over, reversing their positions so that he was the one lying on the hard ground.

As his hands stroked up and down her back and over her hips, molding her body to his, he felt a wave of need so strong that he could not deny it.

Their mouths broke apart so that they could both gasp for breath. Then, tenderly, he drew her lower lip into his mouth, sucking, nibbling, listening to the small sounds of arousal that she made.

She moaned into his mouth, moving her hips against his. He pulled her uniform shirt from her waistband so that he could slip his hands underneath and splay his fingers against her warm skin before fumbling with the catch of her bra.

Frantic for skin-to-skin contact, he eased her a little to the side so that he could push her bra out of the way and cup his hand around one of her breasts, entranced by her softness, the warmth of her skin, and the way her hardened nipple stabbed into his palm, telling him that she was as aroused as he.

She moaned as his other hand cupped her bottom through the uniform pants, pressing her against his erection.

The way she moved her hips in response turned his blood to molten fire.

He heard himself say, "I want you."

And heard her answer, "Yes."

She brought her lips back to his, devouring his mouth.

The world had vanished. Only the two of them existed as he rocked her in his arms, loving the friction that inflamed them both.

"You're wearing too much," he murmured.

She laughed softly. "We can do something about that pretty easily."

He was totally absorbed in her. They might have been the only two people in the universe, until the sound of voices penetrated the haze around them.

Men, coming closer.

On top of him, Sophia stiffened, and Jonah knew then that he'd made a big mistake. While he'd let himself get all wrapped up with her, he'd trapped them between the rubble and the gun-toting guards coming down the trail.

## Chapter Nine

Sophia clamped onto Jonah's hand, feeling her fingers dig into his flesh. What was she thinking? She was supposed to be getting him out of here. Phil had already died in the effort, and now she'd gotten the two of them into a hell of a fix.

Just a little while ago, Jonah had seemed so distant. Then, after the landslide, when he'd wrapped her in his arms, she'd been helpless to stop herself from kissing him. When he'd responded, she'd let her craving to connect with him overcome good sense.

Now they were in deep trouble, and she had to get them to safety. Too bad she had only a superficial knowledge of the cavern's interior, because she'd expected that once they got in here, it would be a straight shot to the other end.

With the voices coming toward them, the logical move would be to go in the other direction. But that way was blocked. Her only option was to take a chance on going back a little way and praying that they found another route.

She grabbed her pack, and they each scrambled for their goggles. Staying low to the ground, she slithered a few yards back, so she could wiggle around the ledge they'd been leaning against when the landslide had struck.

Trusting her judgment, Jonah followed, moving as quietly as a snake.

They made it into a narrow vertical shaft just as she saw lights coming toward them.

She had always hated closed-in places, but she kept going down because her life depended on it.

Jonah came in after her, wedging himself between her and one of the rock walls.

There was only a narrow ledge for them to stand on, and she hated to think how far the drop would be if they lost their footing.

It sounded as if the men who had come down the path were now where she and Jonah had been sitting earlier. There were two of them, and she guessed they were only part of the search party, other men no doubt having taken different routes through the cave, looking for the fugitives.

"That's a hell of a landslide," one of the guards said.

"If they're under that, they're dead."

"Maybe they made it to the other side first."

"I'm going to see how stable it is."

"Okay. But they could still be over here. I'll look around."

His friend made a sound of agreement, and Sophia heard rock crunching.

She felt Jonah moving beside her, doing something at his waist, then raising his arm. Though she wanted to tell him to stay still, there was no way they could talk now.

Above her, she could see a light swing around the area, then move closer.

She wanted to duck her head, but she kept looking up, hoping that the man would miss the tunnel.

Then suddenly a blinding light hit her in the face.

She gasped as the man above them exclaimed, "Got ya."

A boom reverberated in the tunnel. Then another and another.

Even as her ears kept ringing, she knew what had happened. Jonah had fired one of the guns he'd taken from the weapons rack.

The light flicked away from the opening of the shaft, and Jonah pushed past her, scrambling up and disappearing over the rim.

She followed him up, where she saw him leaning over a man lying on the ground.

"Buck?" a voice called.

When she heard rocks sliding around, she knew the other guy was coming. Jonah pulled her down behind the ledge where they'd been sitting.

The sound of tumbling rocks grew louder, and then she heard a scream that faded away as though someone was falling through space.

"Sounds like he went over the edge," Jonah said. "And this one's dead. Still, the shooting and the scream might bring more guys. We've got to get out of here."

"Where?" she asked, hearing her voice tremble.

"Across the rock slide."

"But that guy just slipped and fell on the loose rubble."

"He was in a hurry. We'll be careful."

He sounded confident. Then she remembered why they'd stopped here in the first place. "Your leg."

"It will be okay. We've got to get going."

He had barely finished speaking when they heard more voices behind them—farther away than last time, but coming closer.

"You were right," she whispered. "We drew their attention."

"Unfortunately."

As they put the night-vision goggles back on, he led her quickly toward the rubble. Stepping onto the gravelly surface, he tested his footing, then reached for her hand.

"Don't put your full weight down until you're sure of the surface," he said.

"Okay." Together they started across, leaning over so they could grasp the rocks with their hands and moving cautiously. The voices were getting closer, and she wanted to hurry, but she knew that would be a fatal mistake, given what had happened to the last man who had walked out onto this unstable surface.

They were almost to the other side, when the blinding beam from a flashlight hit them.

"Over there," one of the guards called.

"Keep going," Jonah ordered.

"What about you?"

"I'll be along in a minute," he assured her.

One of the guards spoke up again. "Who the hell is that with him?"

"It looks like the woman who got into the bunker."

"Where the hell did she come from?"

"Who knows. But don't shoot him if you can help it," one of the guards ordered. "Montgomery wants him for questioning."

"Get behind me," Jonah whispered. "Press against the wall on your left."

She did as he asked, knowing she was using him for a shield.

She could see the men trying to line up a shot, but it looked like they couldn't do it with Jonah in the way.

One of the guards started after them across the rubble field, moving too quickly, and the rocks shifted again.

He cursed and slowed down.

Looking back, she saw that Jonah had put a boulder between himself and the men and was digging furiously with his hands.

"What are you doing?" she whispered.

"Loosening this thing. It's big, and not much is holding it in place."

She came around and started helping him.

"Get back."

Ignoring him, she kept digging.

They worked frantically, as one of the guards inched toward them.

Finally, the boulder shifted. "Get back. Now! It's going to go."

This time she followed orders, making it to the other side of the unstable area just as the boulder tumbled down the slope, loosening the whole pile of rocks again.

For a horrible moment, the ground shifted under Jonah's feet, and she thought he was going over the edge. Sophia screamed and grabbed for his hand. Their fingers brushed, but he couldn't hold on. She lunged closer, her hand closing over his, pulling him off the unstable surface. He teetered on solid ground, and she pulled him the rest of the way.

He swore. "You could have gotten killed."

"I couldn't leave you there."

The exchange was interrupted by a scream as the man who had come after them lost his footing and was carried over the edge by the rock fall.

She watched him, feeling sick.

But Jonah didn't give her time to worry about the carnage.

"The whole mess is shifting again. Run!" he shouted.

She ran as rocks rumbled after them. This time the slide sounded bigger than before.

They kept moving down the tunnel at a fast pace, and she knew Jonah's leg must be aching with the strain.

"You need to stop."

"We need to get out of here before they figure out some way to get across."

He was right, but she heard the pain in his voice as he answered her.

Finally she could see light ahead of them and knew they were almost home free.

"Thank God."

But her thanks were short-lived. When she had come this way a few days ago, she and Phil had forded an underground stream. Today it was much deeper and moving faster.

"You have a boat stashed somewhere?" Jonah asked.

"Last time we waded across."

He looked at the fast-flowing stream. About ten feet wide, it was too far to jump across. "We can't wade now."

"But we have to get to the other side."

"Yeah. Let's see what's in your pack."

When she took it off, he rummaged inside and found some supplies. First he pulled out a waterproof bag. It was small, so he sealed the gun and the magazines inside and tucked them into his waistband before pulling a length of rope out of the pack.

After scanning the other side, he cursed under his breath. "There's nothing I can anchor it to." Instead he tied one end around his waist and the other around hers, then looked down the passage where the water disappeared into the gaping darkness.

She followed his gaze and shivered.

"You know where the river comes out?" he asked.

"No."

"In that case, we don't want to get swept away." He reached for her hand. "We should stay close together."

She had no intention of being anywhere else. Locking her fingers with his, she waded into the water with him, testing the current.

The water was cold and it covered their feet, then their knees, then rose to their waists. But the depth was only one problem. The current was another. She struggled to keep her footing as the water came up to her breasts, numbing her from that point downward.

When she wavered, he steadied her. "Okay to keep going?"

"Yes."

Jonah was almost to the other bank when she slipped and went down. She lost her grip on his hand, and her head dipped below the surface. If she hadn't been tied to Jonah, she would have been swept downstream.

He pulled on the rope, reeling her in, then dragged her up and helped her toward the opposite shore.

She gasped, clinging to him, trying not to drag them both to destruction.

"Steady."

"I'm trying," she sputtered.

Somehow they made it to the other side. But now they were downstream where the rock walls made it difficult to climb out. So they had to wade upstream again, against the current, aiming for the cave opening.

It was tough going. When she slipped, she grabbed for Jonah, only her hand went to the pack, pulling it off his shoulder. It bobbed in the water, then disappeared into the darkness.

This time she was the one who cursed.

"It's okay. All we have to do is get to the opening."

She gritted her teeth and concentrated on pushing upstream, knowing the struggle would have been impossible if she were alone. Jonah stayed beside her, and when he finally threw himself onto the shore he pulled her after him.

Flopping onto dry ground, she lay panting beside him.

The cave opening was small and almost hidden by vines trailing down a rock wall. When Jonah pushed the vines aside, the light hurt her eyes. He used a hand for a sunshade and peered into the early-morning sunlight. They were about fifty feet up, on a rock outcropping. Below them, sunlight dappled the new green leaves of tall oak and locust trees.

Jonah turned back to her. "This is the middle of nowhere. But it doesn't look much like Thailand. I'd say spring in the eastern United States."

"Good guess." She wrapped her arms around her wet shoulders. "It's West Virginia."

He gave her an accusing look. "It would have been easy enough for you to tell me that two days ago."

"Like I said, it was safer for you not to know. It might have changed the equation with Montgomery."

He scowled. "Yeah. Maybe I was already being too assertive with him yesterday."

"Like how?"

"I told him a long story about Lieutenant Calley."

She laughed. "I'll bet he loved that."

He glanced back the way they'd come. "I don't suppose you know how that bunker got there?"

"Actually, I do know. It was a fallout shelter left over from the Cold War. For some important government officials."

"How were they supposed to get to West Virginia in case of a nuclear attack?"

"God knows. There's a train line that runs down from D.C. It's not too far from here. Maybe they were supposed to take the Eisenhower Special."

He laughed, which she took as a good sign. She imagined he hadn't had much to laugh about in the past few weeks.

"There's a similar bunker under the Greenbrier Hotel. That one was for members of Congress."

"Another waste of taxpayers' money." He eased back so that his head and shoulders were propped against a rock. She heard him sigh.

"What?"

"I was trying to orient myself. I hate to ask, but what month is this?"

"May. Does that help you figure out a time frame for yourself?"

"Unfortunately, no," he answered in a gritty voice.

"We'll work on getting your real memories back."

"First things first. We've got to get out of here and get some dry clothing."

"Yes."

"How did you find out there was a back way into the bunker?"

"The Light Street guys scrounged up some old plans."

"And you're assuming Montgomery didn't have them," he asked.

She nodded and looked over her shoulder. "I hope not."

"Yeah. But they know you got in through a back door. So even if they don't know this specific exit, they're going to figure out where it is, so let's get going."

Conceding the point, she scrambled to her feet and ducked so that she stepped outside the mouth of the cave. When the wind hit her wet clothing, her teeth started chattering.

Jonah moved to her side, looking down from the rocky promontory. "We're exposed up here. You remember the way down?"

"I hope so." She pointed toward a rock ledge that they could use as an oversized step.

He kept the rope on them, and they climbed steadily downward. She was sure his leg was screaming when they reached the bottom, but he didn't complain.

When they were on level ground, he untied the rope and slung his arm around her shoulder. "Did that Light Street group tell you what to do when you got out of the cave?"

She sighed. "I had a cell phone in a waterproof case. But it was in the pack. I'm sorry. It's gone."

"Don't beat yourself up over it. The important thing is that we got across the river."

"Okay," she answered in a small voice.

"Let's head that way." He pointed to his right.

"Why?"

"It's downhill. Better for the leg."

"Right."

They started walking, and she didn't feel any warmer than when they'd been up on the rocks. It might be May, but the wet clothing felt like ice on her skin.

She tried to clamp her teeth together, but that was too much effort, and she finally gave up and let them click like props in a graveyard movie.

Jonah stayed right beside her as they staggered through the woods, occasionally detouring around patches of brambles or poison ivy or large rock outcroppings.

Too bad the cave entrance was on a rock wall in the middle of nowhere. But that was probably why no one had discovered it. Or maybe they had, but they'd decided it was too inconvenient to develop as a tourist attraction like the other caverns in this part of the country.

As their feet crunched across dry leaves, she started wondering how she was going to keep going. She wanted to sink to the forest floor and cover herself with leaves to get warm.

Jonah urged her along, and if he could keep walking on his mangled leg, she could damn well keep up.

"I'm not much help," she muttered.

His hand tightened on hers. "Oh yeah? If you hadn't risked your life to go into the bunker and get me out, we wouldn't be here now."

"True."

He turned toward her and wrapped her in his arms. She clung to him for long moments, glad of the warmth and the comfort.

"Just a little farther," he said, easing away.

"How do you know?"

"Because we're due for a break."

He knitted his fingers with hers, and they kept walking. She started off with more resolve, but soon her head drooped and her feet shuffled through the leaves and sometimes slid over the rocks. When she stepped into a foot-deep hole filled with water, she almost fell over. Thanks to Jonah she remained upright.

When he stopped short, she made a small sound and looked up.

"Over there." He pointed ahead of them and to the left.

She squinted, trying to follow his gaze. "What is it?"

"A cabin."

"Maybe somebody's home."

"And maybe not."

## *Chapter Ten*

Sophia waited in a stand of trees, leaning against the trunk of a massive oak, while Jonah went to investigate. It was all she could do to stay on her feet now, and she watched him through dull eyes. Wet and cold for too long, she knew she was in trouble if she didn't get inside soon.

When Jonah came back she watched his face anxiously and picked up his look of relief.

"It's an empty hunting cabin." He gave her a concerned look. "Come on."

When she pushed away from the tree, she wavered on her feet.

"Too bad I can't carry you."

"We could carry each other," she mumbled.

He slung his arm around her waist, holding her up as they crossed the fifty yards to the cabin, which was set on blocks, raising it two feet above the forest floor.

She stared stupidly at the open door. "They left it open?"

"No, but they left a key under a rock out front," he said as he helped her up four steps. He closed the door behind them and dropped a length of wood that acted as a bolt into a slot, sealing them inside.

She looked around, registering a simple and homey interior,

with a fireplace of local rocks against one wall and a double bed with a metal frame opposite. The warm quilt drew her eyes.

"Take off your clothes and get under the covers," Jonah told her. "I'm going to make a fire."

She staggered to the bed and plopped down, but that was as far as she got. Too tired to undress, she kicked off her shoes, lay down and closed her eyes, listening to Jonah moving around.

She dozed until he shook her gently. "Can you get undressed?"

"I don't think so."

Sitting her up, he peeled off her wet shirt and pants, then her bra. She might have been embarrassed that she was almost naked in front of him, her nipples drawn into tight points by the cold, but she was too tired to make the effort.

He left her damp panties on, then moved her aside to pull down the blankets and help her under.

As she snuggled into the warmth of the bed, she could see a fire crackling and realized he must have made it while she was dozing.

"Come to bed," she whispered.

"I will, but I've got a couple of things to do."

She watched him through slitted eyes, seeing he had exchanged his wet shirt and pants for others he must have found in the cabin. They looked too big.

She was sure his leg must be beyond painful, but he kept moving around. He laid their wet clothing on the back and seat of a rocker by the fireplace where it would dry. Then he went outside. Her heart pounding, she waited for him to return. A few minutes later he came back with more wood and an ax.

She dozed again, then woke when she heard him doing something in the corner of the room. She tried to sit up and see what was going on, but all she could manage was a question.

"What?"

"Just go to sleep."

"Um."

She watched him take the SIG out of the waterproof pouch and replace the clip with a full one before setting it on the table by the bed. Then he stripped off his borrowed clothing and climbed under the covers.

It felt as if an ice cube had joined her.

"You're cold."

"Sorry."

He scooted away from her.

"I didn't mean to complain." She used the last of her energy to roll toward him, sling her arm over his chest and press her face to his shoulder.

"We're safe," she murmured.

"Let's hope so." He cleared his throat. "Those guys in uniform, they're not regular army, are they?"

"No. They're from a private military group. Like Blackwater."

"Montgomery hired them?"

"Not sure." She couldn't manage any more conversation. Her eyes were already closed, and she drifted off to sleep.

Some time later, she was sucked into a dream. It started off with a hazy warmth that heated her all the way to her bones. She and Jonah were finally together again after all the years of separation, and the feeling of relief was like a living thing.

They were both naked, lying together in a cozy bed. She clung to him, kissing him deeply, running her hands over his back and shoulders. She wanted to tell him how much she'd missed him, how her life had been incomplete without him. Before she could speak the words, an enormous wind came pounding at them, dragging them apart.

"Jonah?"

He was gone. Panic gripped her as she tried to find him. Then she was running through the woods—wet and cold and search-

ing desperately for him. Only she was being pursued by men in
blue uniforms who were determined to keep her from him.

"No," she moaned.

"Sophia!"

He called her name, but his voice came from a long way
away.

One of the men caught up with her and grabbed her, and she tried
to fight him off, but he captured her flailing arms and held her still.

She kept fighting with all her strength, because she knew she
had to get back to Jonah.

His voice reached her again.

"Easy. Take it easy."

"No!"

"Sophia, wake up."

Her eyes blinked open, and she looked up into Jonah's face.
He was pressing her against the mattress while he held her arms,
and she knew that she must have been hitting him.

"Oh Lord, did I hurt you?" she gasped.

"It's okay."

"I'm sorry."

"You were dreaming."

They had been naked in the dream, and they were almost
naked now. She felt his muscular leg against hers, his hip pressed
to her thigh.

But it was obvious his mind wasn't in the same place as hers.

"We can't stay here too long. In case they figure out where
we are."

She kept her gaze fixed on him. "Don't we have a little time?"
She didn't say why she wanted more time. She simply wrapped
her arms around him and pulled him to her. This was like the
dream. They were warm and cozy and finally together again
after so many years of separation.

Unlike in the dream, his body had stiffened.

"Sophia…" His voice held the sound of refusal.

"Don't deny us what we both want so much. Come here."

He made a strangled sound as he cradled her against himself. At the same time, his mouth came down on hers for a hot, thirsty kiss. The taste of him was familiar and heady.

Electricity arced between them as past and present merged. She remembered that night so long ago and all the emotions he had kindled in her—emotions that she hadn't dared to share with him because that made her too vulnerable.

She had thought nothing in her life could ever be that good again. But here he was, back in her arms, and it was everything she had dreamed of.

She opened for him, telling him with her mouth and body and hands that slid over his shoulders and down his back that she was his for the taking.

He lifted his mouth a fraction. He was breathing hard, yet his words tore at her.

"You should be afraid of me."

She kept her gaze locked with his. "Why?"

"My mind's a mess."

"I understand why you feel that way. You've been through a terrible experience."

"It's not over."

"It will be. You grew up tough. You know how to cope."

His face hardened. "I grew up tough and no good."

"Don't say that. You turned into a man who should be proud of the life he's made for himself."

"How do you know?"

"Like I said, I read about your career. You went on some amazing missions."

"That was then. This is now."

"Jonah, don't sell yourself short. Even when you don't remember specifics, it's obvious that you're drawing on the training you got in the Special Forces. If you need it, you reach for it, and it's there."

When he only stared at her, she went on.

"I may have had the trail markers, but you were the one who got us out of that cave, across the river and through the woods to this cabin. You have most of what you need, and we'll get the rest of it back."

"How?"

"We can start by getting in touch with more of your memories." She struggled to keep her voice steady. "Like memories of that night."

"Which night?"

"Don't pretend you don't remember."

She knew from his expression that he knew exactly what night she meant.

"I missed you so much," she whispered, then knew she had given a lot away. Maybe too much. If he didn't feel the same, something inside her would shrivel and die.

She waited with the breath frozen in her lungs.

"Oh yes."

He gathered her to him again, and she sighed out her relief.

He brought her mouth back to his, sending heat coursing through her. Sliding her hands down his body, she cupped his buttocks, pulling his erection against her thigh.

He made a low sound, and she thought for a moment that he would tear off her panties and his shorts and plunge into her.

Instead he rolled to his side, taking her with him so that they were facing each other on the bed.

Outside, sunlight filtered through the trees and seeped through the window. He looked into her eyes, sliding his hands through her hair, then kissing her gently as he stroked his fingers over her cheeks, down to her jaw and over her collarbones.

She touched his body with the same tenderness, awed to be playing her fingers over his broad chest, burrowing into the thick dark hair she found there, then grinning as she drew circles around his flat nipples and heard his quick, indrawn breath.

"You like that," she murmured.

"You know I do."

He pulled the covers down so that he could see her breasts. They weren't quite as firm as they had been ten years ago, and she had a moment of uncertainty.

But his tender look told her what she needed to know. He sighed as he cradled them in his hands, stroking his thumbs across the tightened nipples.

"I love the way you feel."

"That's so good. What you're doing is so good."

He bent his head, circling one tight peak with his tongue, then sucking it into his mouth while he plucked at the other with his thumb and finger.

She heard herself make a sobbing sound as the pleasure of it surged through her.

They were almost naked, but the two thin layers of clothing between them had become intolerable.

She reached down, finding the waistband of her panties so she could push them over her hips and down her legs, where she kicked them away.

Seeing what she was doing, he followed her example. When they were both naked, he grinned at her, then sobered as he reached down to touch her intimately, his fingers tangling in the triangle of blond hair at the top of her legs before slipping lower, into the wet heat between her legs.

The way he caressed her said volumes. She knew that he remembered what she liked. His finger dipped inside her, then moving all the way up to the site of her greatest sensation before traveling downward and starting all over again.

The pleasure was exquisite. She wanted to give him that same joy, but when she reached down the front of his body, he stopped her hand before she found her goal.

"Don't." He caught his breath. "I need you too much."

"No more than I need you."

When he stroked her again, heat and raw emotion surged through her, and she heard his ragged breathing mingling with hers.

"I want you inside me. Now."

She rolled to her back and held out her arms to him. Finally, he covered her body with his and plunged inside her.

Sexual need surged between them. At the same time, she felt that an old wound was finally healed.

He brought his mouth back to her, his kiss hot and greedy as he moved in a steady rhythm, plunging into her and withdrawing.

Even as her need for release spiraled out of control, she felt him holding back, waiting for her to reach the peak.

She climbed to the top of the mountain, then toppled over the edge. As she did, she felt him follow her.

The intensity of her climax brought a cry to her lips, and his voice joined hers as he shouted his pleasure, then he collapsed on top of her and lay breathing hard and fast.

Wanting to keep him close, she stroked his damp shoulders and kissed his cheek.

When he started to move, she tightened her hold on him.

"I'm going to crush you," he whispered.

"No. I like the feel of your weight on top of me."

He stayed a few moments longer, then kissed her once more before rolling to his side, clasping her to him.

She snuggled against him, still trying to absorb the reality of this reunion. He had made wonderful love to her, and she felt as though the years of separation had been wiped away. But she knew it was only an illusion.

She knew too that he wasn't going to be satisfied with himself until he remembered everything—not just making love with her.

His hand glided to the back of her thigh, and he touched the small mole just below her butt. "I remember that," he murmured.

"Yes. You thought it was cute."

He brought her back to the present with his next words. Practical words.

"We need to eat."

In response, her stomach growled.

"You're hungry."

"I hadn't even thought about food." She turned toward the window. "Is this lunch or dinner?"

"I'm not sure."

"Are you going to go out and shoot a wild turkey?"

He laughed. "With a SIG? I don't think so. But I checked the kitchen area. There's some food we can steal. Maybe we can leave some money."

"Where would we get it?"

His face twisted. "I liberated some money from Montgomery. His lieutenant had a stack of bills in his desk drawer."

"How did you find it?"

"It was after my last session. Montgomery was in his office, and his lieutenant was away from his desk, so I did some poking around."

"That was taking a chance."

"Yeah." He climbed casually out of bed, giving her a nice view of his magnificent body. Without bothering to find his pants, he walked across the room to a kitchen area with cabinets, a sink and what looked like a wood-burning stove.

He might be comfortable naked, but she walked to the chair and quickly pulled on her pants and shirt he'd dried in front of the fire.

Reaching up, he opened one of the cabinets and got some bottled water, then followed with some cellophane-wrapped packages.

When he turned back with the food in his hands, he saw that she'd pulled on her clothes and straightened the bedcovers before sitting with her back against the headboard.

"Are we getting formal?" he asked.

"Decent."

He put the food on the bed, then grabbed his pants from the chair and put them on. After plumping up his pillow, he sat back down.

She picked up one of the bottles of water, giving him a sideways look. They had just made love. Now they were sharing a meal, and that felt almost as intimate.

She wanted to talk about the two of them, but she didn't want to push him into a discussion he wasn't ready for. Not when they'd just found each other again. The connection was too new—and too fragile. She wasn't going to kid herself. He could pull away from her if she didn't handle this right. So she let him set the pace.

Pointing to the packages on the bed, he said, "We've got beef jerky, peanut butter crackers and apricot leather."

"What's that?"

"Ground-up fruit mixed with sugar and hardened. It's pretty good."

He opened one of the beef sticks and handed it to her. "Excellent protein. But you've got to have good teeth."

"I do."

She tried some of the meat, then took a swallow of water. He did the same and opened the peanut butter crackers.

They focused on the simple meal, but she sensed tension building inside him.

After a sip of water, he cleared his throat. "I guess the first thing we need to do is figure out what Dr. Montgomery thinks I know."

## *Chapter Eleven*

Jonah waited with his breath frozen in his lungs. Dinner—or was it lunch?—had been a way of stalling.

When they had made love, he had trusted Sophia with his emotions. Now he had dared to confront her with the problem that held him in its iron grip.

She laid her hand lightly over his. "We don't have to do it all at once," she murmured.

"Yeah, but the longer I can't access my memories, the more threat I am to you."

"Why are you a threat?"

"Because Montgomery wants information from me. And if his guys catch up with me, we're a hell of a lot better off if I have the big picture."

She knitted her fingers with his. "We can start with easy stuff. Let's do some more of what we tried before."

"Which is?"

"I'll tell you about your life, and you'll see if what I say triggers more memories.

"Okay."

She closed her eyes, thinking for a moment.

"What are you trying to do—dredge up something good?"

"I'm trying to see what's most effective." She squeezed his hand. "Do you remember the fireworks incident?"

"Not in those words."

"Do you remember Arty Hillman?"

He blinked as a pudgy face leaped into his mind. "The fat kid with the crew cut?"

"Yes."

"What about him?"

"Try to put that together with fireworks."

He closed his eyes, and suddenly a memory was there. Arty Hillman at twilight, out in a field, setting off fireworks—and a bunch of kids including Sophia and Jonah watching.

"A Roman candle fell over as it started to go off, shooting balls of fire toward the crowd."

"Good job."

He shrugged. "Okay. I'm remembering stuff from school. Does that mean whatever Montgomery was drugging me with is out of my system?"

"I hope so. But I don't know what it was. What else do you remember about the fireworks?"

"A fireball hit Danny Vera," Jonah said.

"And…"

"And I ran over and threw him on the ground and smothered the fire."

"Right. You got your arm burned, as I remember."

"Yeah."

Her hand tightened on his. "Everybody else scattered, but you ran toward Danny. When you threw him down, two fireballs flew over your head."

"I heard them," he whispered.

"Nobody had cell phones back then. One of the guys ran to the pay phone at a gas station and called 911."

"Yes. They took him to the hospital in an ambulance. But I wouldn't go," he finished.

"Why not?"

"Because I was afraid they were going to charge me for treatment, and I knew my mom didn't have the money."

"So you went around with blisters on your arm."

He winced. "They hurt like hell."

"Do you remember anything else connected with the incident?"

"My mom got mad because my shirt was ruined."

"You were a hero, and that was her focus?"

He shrugged. "After my dad died, we didn't have a lot of money. Every penny counted. That's why I don't like remembering that I kept the money I earned at my job and spent it on myself."

"Most kids would have done that."

"I should have given some to Mom."

"Did you make it up to her later?"

"Yeah. I bought her a condo in Daytona Beach."

"You're allowed to feel good about that."

He nodded.

"What else do you remember about your family?"

"I had an older sister. She got married right out of high school and moved away. We didn't see much of her after that, but I gather she was in an abusive relationship." He shrugged. "No wonder I wanted to forget all of that."

"But you're doing good bringing it back."

He snorted. "I've tried to bury all that stuff."

"What do you remember about my family?" she asked in a low voice.

He turned his head toward her, then looked across the room, his eyes unfocused. "Your background was a lot different from mine. Your dad was the president of the local bank, and your mom spent a lot of her time playing tennis at Turf Valley Country Club. They wouldn't have liked to know you spent the night with me."

Sophia felt her stomach knot, hating to let his judgment stand. "They were decent people," she said, defending them. "My mom also raised money for the Humane Society. And she spent a lot of time doing her own gardening."

"And if she needed help with the heavy work, she could ask someone from the lawn service."

"Are you faulting her for that?"

"I'm just pointing out that she had more choices than my mom."

"We both know that."

"What happened to your parents?" he suddenly asked.

Her voice lowered. "You didn't hear about it?"

His gaze sharpened. "What did I miss?"

"My dad was flying my mom and my little sister back to college. He ran into bad fog and crashed into a house. They were all killed. Luckily nobody was in the house."

He winced and took her hand again. "Sophia, I'm so sorry. I never heard about it. How old were you?"

"I was twenty-two. My family was wiped out. Then it turned out there were some things wrong with their will, and I had to fight my aunt and uncle for control of the estate."

"I didn't know."

"You were long gone."

"Yeah."

"There's something I want to tell you."

The way she said it put him on alert. "Something bad?"

"Yes." She looked like a swimmer plunging off the high board when she said, "I was lonely and adrift after they died. I got into a relationship—with a guy who seemed like he could make me happy. When things started going bad, I wondered if he'd been in love with me or my money."

"Your boyfriend?"

She cleared her throat. "My husband."

He stared at her. It was none of his business. Still, he couldn't help feeling as though she'd stuck an ice pick between his ribs. But what had he expected—that after the night they'd spent together, she'd become a nun? He certainly hadn't given up sex after that. But he hadn't gotten into any serious relationships, either.

She was still speaking, and he strove to listen above the roaring in his ears.

"I knew within a year that I'd made a big mistake. But I stuck with it another year. I ended up giving him a cash settlement."

"I'm sorry."

"I learned my lesson." Her face changed. "But I didn't need to tell you all that."

"Apparently, you did."

"I guess I wanted it out in the open."

"You don't owe me any explanations."

"I felt like I did." She huffed out a breath, then said, "Let's get back on track. We got into your early life, but what about later? What about the army? What do you remember about that?"

He leaned back and closed his eyes, inviting memories. To his relief, they came—clear and crisp—telling him that his brain was no longer muzzy.

"I remember basic training. I remember Ranger training. I remember…a lot of assignments."

"What about them?"

"Most of them are classified. But you read about them anyway." A thought struck him. "How did the Light Street people get hold of my classified records?"

"I guess they have connections. But let's keep this focused on you. You remember details you didn't remember the other night?"

"Yes." He gave her a fierce look. "I can account for my time—until a few months ago."

"Do you remember leaving for Afghanistan?"

"No."

She looked down at their joined hands. "So a lot of stuff has come back to you, but not that."

"Yeah. Why not? Does it have something to do with the drugs?"

"Maybe. Or maybe it was so traumatic that you don't want to deal with it."

He nodded. "So I'm stuck."

"We could try hypnosis."

As she made the suggestion, he felt his face go hard.

"Montgomery wanted to try hypnosis."

"That doesn't make us alike."

He answered with a tight nod. But he still hadn't liked hearing the suggestion. "It makes me vulnerable," he managed to say.

She kept her gaze fixed on him. "Yes. So what about it?"

CARLTON MONTGOMERY stared at the computer screen, reading his latest e-mail. The message made the back of his neck prickle. According to his correspondent, it was his fault that the bunker was vulnerable to invasion. His fault that Baker had escaped. And he'd damn well better get the man back.

He'd done his best. But who in hell could have predicted that two people would have shown up to spring Major Baker?

The guards had killed a man in a rock-hewn tunnel outside the developed part of the bunker. But there was apparently another person involved. Graves had seen her and said it was a woman.

So why had she volunteered for what could have turned into a suicide mission?

Maybe she was doing it for money. Maybe she believed in the

cause. Or maybe she was personally involved. That was an interesting angle and probably worth pursuing.

A knock at the door made him sit up straighter and switch the screen to another window. "Come."

Lieutenant Olson walked into the room.

"Have you found him?" Montgomery demanded.

"Not yet. But it looks like we've lost four men."

Montgomery kept his face impassive. "They didn't report back?"

"Patterson got shot by the guy who covered Baker and the woman's exit. Scottinger and Marks were on the search team. We found Scottinger's body. No sign of Marks."

"He could be lost in the cave."

"He doesn't answer his comm unit. And some of the men saw Templeton go over the edge of a cliff in a landslide inside the cave."

"Do you have any good news?"

"The cave is huge, but we know how the woman and the other man found their way through it. They laid a trail, using infrared markers."

"And?"

"We're following the trail. When we get to the end, we'll know where they exited the cave. And when we know that, we'll know where to search."

The information gave him a glimmer of hope, but he kept his voice hard. "What makes you think they're still in the area?"

"Baker's leg was injured. He can't walk all that far. We'll get him."

JONAH STARED at Sophia for long moments, and she kept her gaze steady. He needed to know what had wiped out his memory of the past few months and he needed to know whatever facts were now hidden from him.

So what were his options? He could trust her. Or he could go it alone. Too bad he felt as if he was trying to play poker with a rigged deck.

He sighed. "All right."

"You're sure?"

"No."

"Thanks for being honest. But it won't work unless you trust me enough to let me put you under."

"Yeah."

He watched her climb off the bed and walk to the fireplace, where she grabbed the rocking chair and carried it over.

"What do you want me to do?" he asked.

"Make yourself comfortable. You can prop yourself up with both pillows. I'll sit over here and give you suggestions."

"Okay." He stacked the pillows, then lay down with his arms rigidly at his sides.

"Relax."

"Easier said than done."

"Hypnosis is a way to go back and visit a threatening experience. But you won't really be there."

"So what good does it do me?"

"You'll be observing. You can watch it happening on a big television screen. And you can change the date to this time and place any time you want to."

"How?"

"You just have to tell me 'I need to leave this place.'"

"Okay."

"And if I need to wake you, we'll have a trigger phrase. 'Jonah, wake up now.'"

He kept his gaze focused on her. "You're sure that will work?"

She kept her eyes steady as she looked back. "Yes. So, shall we go ahead?"

He dragged in a breath and let it out slowly. "Yes."

"Good. A convenient way to do it is to look up to the line where the ceiling meets the top of the wall. Why don't you do that now?"

He took the suggestion, wondering what good it would do.

"Relax…now. Relax…now," she said, her voice calm and soothing. "Across the room is a big television set. It's one of those expensive flat screens. Sixty-inch. It takes up a big part of the wall in this small cabin. You're going to watch a movie about the life of Jonah Baker. Do you see the screen?"

"Yes," he answered, because he did. It seemed very wide and solid.

"You can see yourself on the television. You won't be there, but you can watch what happened. You're not involved. You're only an observer. All right?"

"Yes."

"You're back in school. Eighth grade."

"Okay."

"You're in the cafeteria. With your friends Roger and Kevin."

"Yes."

"It's the day Jeff Bolton lost his retainer."

He laughed. "He took off his retainer at lunch and wrapped it in his napkin. I can see him throwing it in the trash by accident. Now he's digging through the garbage looking for it."

"Does he find it?"

"Yeah. And he had to take a shower before they'd let him back into class."

"Good. Let's move forward. To the year after you graduated from high school. It's six weeks into basic training. You're still watching on TV. You're not really there. Do you see yourself?"

"Yes."

"Where is basic training?"

"Fort Bragg."

"And now you're in the mess hall, getting breakfast."

"Yes."

"Who are your friends?"

"Costa and Stevenson."

"So you're eating with them."

"Yes."

"Any time you want to stop watching yourself and come back to this place and time, just say, 'I want to come back.' And you will."

"Okay."

"In basic training, what's your best skill?"

"I'm good on the firing range. And on the obstacle course. I have the record for the shortest time."

"Good. So you're trying to keep that record. Who's the next fastest guy?"

"Wolinsky."

"You're going up against Wolinsky. You're going to try your damnedest to beat him again."

"Yes." On the screen he was watching himself back there in the hot fields, crawling under barbed wire, then scrambling up and running through a nest of tires. Wolinsky was right behind him. They got to the rope-and-barrier climb and after Jonah almost lost his grip, he pulled himself up, then vaulted over the wooden barrier and let himself fall to the straw on the other side. He picked himself up and ran the last fifty yards to the finish line, with Wolinsky puffing along right behind him.

"I made it. Ahead of him."

"Do you feel good?"

"Yeah. I'm good at this. Good at army stuff. Not like back in school when I had to be…a rebel to make myself stand out."

"That's why you did it?"

"Yeah."

"You could have done better in school if you'd wanted?"

"Yes. And I learn fast in basic training. I think they're going to ask if I want to join the Rangers."

"Good."

"Let's move forward. Your first assignment."

"Germany."

"Do you like it there?"

"It's cold and rainy. But the beer is good, and the women like American soldiers. They think they can get us to marry them and take them home. I won't be here long. It's only temporary duty for me. I'm going to Iraq next. We're going to be training their military."

"Let's move forward again. You're going to Afghanistan."

He shifted on the bed. He'd felt safe and relaxed, watching himself on television, but now he felt unsettled.

"It's all right. You're not there. You're only watching on television. Can you see the scene on the television?"

"Yes."

"That's good. It's safe to watch it on television. You're learning about the assignment. Who's briefing you?"

"Colonel Luntz."

"What does he look like?"

"He's tall. He holds himself very straight. Dark hair with some gray. A scar cutting his left eyebrow. He's lucky he didn't lose his eye."

"What's he saying?"

Frustration made his voice sharp. "I should be able to hear him, but I can't."

"That's okay. Try to tune in on him."

"I can't."

"Who else is there?"

"The guys on the team. Hall. Shredder. Fromer." As he said that name, a wave of cold swept over him.

"Jonah, what?"

"He's getting out of his seat. He's coming toward me. He's got a gun. No—"

"Who?"

"Fromer." His heart was pounding now, and sweat beaded on his forehead. "Stay away from me, you bastard," he shouted as he looked for a way to defend himself. He lunged for the gun on the bedside table.

# Chapter Twelve

Sophia gasped as Jonah surged off the bed, his expression fierce. Afraid he was going to grab her, she reared back in the chair, almost knocking it over, then went rigid as he snatched up the gun and whirled to face her, holding the weapon in a two-handed grip, pointing it at her chest where she still sat, trying to stop the chair from rocking.

When he spoke, his tone was hard and direct. "I've had enough. Stay away from me, you bastard."

When she saw the murder in his eyes and heard the coldness in his voice, terror threatened to swamp her.

She'd hypnotized other people before, and nothing like this had ever happened. It *shouldn't* have happened.

The process had been working fine. She'd taken him back to school, then to basic training and then through his first assignment. Then something had gone terribly wrong.

*Stay calm,* she ordered herself. Speaking slowly and directly, she gave him the trigger phrase that they had agreed on. "Jonah, wake up. Wake up now."

She had told him that the trigger would work. It always had worked when she had hypnotized a client in the past.

Now nothing was going according to plan. He didn't seem to

hear her, and to her horror, he took a step toward her, still holding the weapon pointed at her chest.

She stayed where she was, her gaze glued to him—and the gun in his hands. She wanted to run, but deep in her consciousness, she knew that trying to get away would be exactly the wrong move. Showing fear would be fatal.

It took every scrap of determination she possessed to keep her voice steady and even as she faced this man she thought she knew.

"Jonah, wake up. Wake up now."

Totally ignoring anything she said, he whispered, "You did it, damn you."

"No. It wasn't me. I'm not—" In her desperation, she had spoken automatically, but she stopped herself before she could say the man's name. That was exactly the wrong thing to do. Maybe hearing the name of his enemy would make him pull the trigger.

"Jonah, it's Sophia. Wake up. I'm Sophia Rhodes. We're in the cabin that we found after we escaped from the cave."

His gaze was still fixed, but she detected something different in his eyes.

"I'll kill you," he repeated, but this time he didn't sound quite so sure of his mission, and she wondered if she was making progress? Or was that just wishful thinking?

All she could do was keep speaking to him, hoping to make a connection. "I'm Sophia. You don't want to kill me. You'd be killing the wrong person. I'm Sophia." When he didn't respond, she went on. "I wasn't at the briefing. I'm Sophia Rhodes, and we're in the cabin that we found in the woods."

The gun came up a few inches, pointed at her head. Sweat drenched his forehead and his skin had turned a pasty shade of white. "I…."

She gripped the arms of the chair, bracing for the worst. He could pull the trigger and shoot her, and he wouldn't even know who he was killing—until she was slumped in the chair. And then what would happen to him?

He was already in trouble. Either the guards from the bunker would get him or the police. Then who would help him figure out what had happened?

Her mouth was so dry that she could hardly speak. But she managed to say, "Jonah, wake up now."

The trigger phrase still didn't seem to be working, so she tried a different approach.

"Jonah, this is Sophia. You're holding a gun on me. But you don't want to shoot me. We made love a little while ago. You care about me. Put the gun down. Wake up now and put the gun down."

He shook his head, looking confused, his eyes darting from her to the interior of the cabin, and she thought he might finally be taking in his surroundings.

"Jonah, wake up now."

He opened his mouth and closed it again. The gun wavered. Then he lowered his arms. But he was still holding the weapon in his right hand.

"Put the gun down," she said. "Jonah, wake up now. Wake up now."

He went very still, his gaze turned inward. Then he raised his head, looking around again. This time she thought he was seeing his surroundings. Eons passed before his gaze came back to her.

"Sophia?"

"Thank God. You're back with me. Jonah, put the gun down."

He looked at the gun in his hand as though he'd just realized he was holding on to a poisonous snake.

With a strangled sound, he carefully set the SIG down on the table where he'd found it.

"What happened?" he whispered, looking from her to the gun and back again.

She swallowed, wondering what she was going to say now that she finally had his attention.

When she didn't speak, he asked, "Was…was I going to shoot you?"

She managed to speak around the lump clogging her windpipe. "No."

His expression turned dark. "Then why was I holding the gun on you?"

She took a step toward him, and he stepped quickly back. "Stay away. It's obvious I'm dangerous."

She couldn't let him think that she was afraid of him. Not now. When his legs hit the edge of the bed, she hurried forward and wrapped him tightly in her embrace, pressing her face against his broad chest. He felt real and solid and she knew that they had just come through a nightmare together. His nightmare.

Still, he remained stiffly in her embrace. "How can you stand to get near me?"

She stroked her hands up and down his back. "Because…" *Because I love you.* She knew that was the truth, but she thought that would be too threatening for him to hear at the moment. Maybe it would always be too threatening.

Instead, as she continued to caress his shoulders, she said, "I care about you. Very much."

He wouldn't even accept that much from her. "Apparently that's a big mistake."

"Don't say that. You're upset."

When she tried to hold him, he broke away, his eyes blazing.

"You're damn right I'm upset. I could have killed you. You damn well know it. Tell me what the hell was going on a few minutes ago."

"Okay. Just take it easy. We'll figure out what happened…"

"Don't hand me a load of psychologist bull. Just tell me why I blinked awake and found out I could have shot you!"

"Do you remember that I hypnotized you?"

"Yes."

"You remember the scenes you watched?"

"School. Basic training. Germany," he answered.

"Then we were talking about the briefing before you shipped out for Afghanistan."

"I remember," he said in a low voice. His gaze locked with hers. "With Colonel Luntz."

"Good."

"He was the guy who gave us the information about the mission."

"Do you remember the mission?"

His gaze turned inward again and she could see he was straining to bring the scene into focus. After half a minute, his face contorted. "No!"

"Okay. Don't get upset."

His jaw hardened. "Don't tell me what to feel. Just tell me what happened next—because I sure as hell don't know. Luntz is the last thing I remember. He was standing in front of a screen with a light pen in his hand. I guess he was doing a Power Point presentation, but I don't remember what he said."

"You said someone named Fromer was there."

"Fromer. I remember him. He was a hothead. I knew he was trouble the minute I saw him."

"In the scene at the briefing, he apparently attacked you. Could that have really happened?"

He flapped his hand in frustration. "I don't know."

"You said, 'You did it.' What did that mean?"

He answered with a curse. "I don't know! All I know is that I went for the gun. Well, I don't *know* that. What I remember is waking up with the gun in my hand."

"I should have put it away."

"No. We had it there for protection. We need the gun. You weren't expecting anything like that, were you?"

"No."

He shifted his weight from one foot to the other. "Anybody else go berserk on you during hypnosis?"

"You didn't go berserk."

"Oh yeah, what would you call it?"

"I don't know. Something…unusual happened to you."

He snorted. "You're trying to put the best possible face on this. But the truth is I'm sick and dangerous, whether or not my mind is free of the damn medication. You should be running in the other direction as fast as you can."

She shook her head. "Don't put the worst possible interpretation on it. Or to put it another way—stop assigning blame."

"What do you want me to do?"

The light had grown dim in the cabin, and she wanted to see his face more clearly. She thought about getting up and lighting one of the oil lamps that sat on the shelf, but she stayed where she was because she didn't want to interrupt, not at such a critical point in their conversation. They were close to some vital information—if they could just figure out how to do it.

She reached out a hand toward him and watched him follow the movement with his eyes.

"Let's try to figure out what part Fromer played in what happened to you. Maybe the incident between you took place in Afghanistan and not where you were being briefed."

"We were in Maryland for the briefing."

"Ah. Another fact. Do you remember exactly where?"

"Somewhere out in the country. I…remember thinking that it looked like an abandoned location. But inside it had been… modernized."

"What does that mean?"

"I guess that they wanted it to look like a dump on the outside, so no one would think they were using the interior."

"Good. What else?"

He sighed. "I can picture the briefing room. A table at the front. Chairs. A computer. A screen." He waved his arm. "But I can't remember anything Luntz said."

"But you came up with the location."

"Like I said. Nothing else," he bit out. "And I assume you're not crazy enough to insist on trying hypnosis again to dig it out of me, right?"

Though her chest felt tight, she had to agree with him. "Right."

"So what's next?"

"I'm not sure," she admitted, wondering if some other technique would trigger the same response. Although she hated to admit it, she was going to have to tread carefully now. But she didn't want to explain that to him.

He gave her an assessing look, and she wondered if he was reading her mind. As he waited for her response, he ran a hand through his hair and finally turned away from her.

She kept her gaze on him, and when he went rigid, she was immediately on guard.

Then she realized he was looking at something outside the window.

"What is it?"

He spoke in a harsh whisper. "I saw a shadow flicker through the trees."

"A deer?"

"No. Someone on two legs. There's a person out there." As he spoke, he moved to the wall.

"Who?" she asked, unconsciously lowering her voice.

"If we're lucky, it could be the guy who owns the cabin." He slipped along the wall, then along to the window, where he peered out.

"Shit."

"What?"

"I see one of the guards from the bunker, dressed in a hunting outfit. If he's here, there are more of them."

Suddenly, she couldn't draw in a full breath. "What are we going to do?"

"Get out of here."

She looked wildly around. As far as she could see, there was only one door to the cabin.

"We can't go out the front door."

"No." He gave her a quick inspection. "Take off that uniform and put these on."

He crossed to the closet and pulled out jeans and a work shirt. She pulled them on and then rolled up the pants legs. He put on a shirt; then he walked to the corner of the room and pulled up two floorboards. She remembered he'd been doing something in the corner while she was lying in bed cold and exhausted. She hadn't known what. Now she saw that he'd chopped a hole in the floor.

As soon as he'd removed the boards, he returned to the closet and pulled out a brown jacket. "Put this on, too. It will blend with the leaves on the ground."

When she complied, he came back to the wall, looking out the window again without showing more than a sliver of his face.

"How close is he?"

"He's holding his position. We've got a little time." He handed her the gun and she wrapped her fingers around the butt.

"Go down through the floor. There's a crawl space under the cabin. Stay flat to the ground. I'll be there as fast as I can."

Her heart was pounding as she lowered herself into the hole

and lay flat on the damp soil, clutching the gun and smelling the musty odor of earth that hadn't dried out in a long time.

Earlier, when the guards had been after them, they must have had orders to kill her and capture Jonah. What were their orders now?

Above her, she could hear him walking rapidly around, obviously making some kind of preparations he'd had in mind all along, in case the guards found them.

She turned her head toward the hole, watching and waiting for him to join her. The seconds ticked by, and she imagined the man outside and the others closing in on the cabin.

Above her, she heard the sound of breaking glass. She wanted to call out to Jonah, but she knew she had to stay quiet. Instead, she only took her lower lip between her teeth and bit down to focus herself. Finally, his feet dangled through the hole, and she let out the breath she'd been holding.

"Stay down!" he ordered in a harsh whisper as he crawled toward her and covered her body with his.

"What?"

Before he could answer the question, she saw flames flickering in the opening above them.

## Chapter Thirteen

"Sorry about the cabin," Jonah muttered. "Maybe the DOD will pay for it."

"What did you do?"

He answered in a harsh whisper that was barely audible above the roaring sound rising above them. "Sprinkled kerosene around the cabin. Then I lit an oil lamp and smashed it into the corner."

"Why?"

He kept his voice low. "To create a diversion. They don't know we could get out through the floor. All they'll see is the burning cabin and they'll think we're inside."

She looked back toward the opening and saw flames licking at the floorboards.

Outside, Jonah's maneuver was having the desired effect.

"Fire," one of the men shouted. "The damn place is on fire."

"They're in there," said another voice. "I didn't see them come out."

She could hear someone pounding on the door.

"Open up. Open the damn door," the same guy shouted, his voice rising with his fear.

"They're busy trying to get inside. Come on," Jonah whispered. Slithering along the ground, he reached the edge of the cabin, and looked out. Above them, flames were creeping up the wall. And now she could hardly hear anything else above the roaring of the fire. It felt as if the whole structure was going to explode. And if it did, fire would come raining down on them.

At the front of the building, she could hear the men still trying to get in.

Someone cried out, and she wondered if they were in trouble, but she had to worry about herself now. The floor above her was hot to the touch, and she heard pops and cracks in the wood.

The whole thing could come crashing down on them at any minute.

Jonah slithered out, keeping to the ground for several yards, then standing up and bending over as he made for the woods.

She exited after him, imitating his stance and following the same route, running for the thick underbrush a hundred yards from the cabin.

Jonah was way ahead of her, and as she hurried to catch up, she hit a patch of rocky ground and went sprawling. She lay there for a minute, catching her breath. When she started to rise, she saw a pair of feet and legs in front of her.

"Hold it right there."

A sick feeling rose in her throat, but with no other option, she flopped back to the ground. When she found a large stone under her hand, she closed her fingers around it.

The man's expression was menacing. "You're the chick who got into the bunker. Who are you?"

She shrugged. "Nobody."

"We'll find that out later. What the hell happened back there? Where's Baker?"

"I don't know. Maybe he's still in the cabin," she answered. "All I wanted to do was get out."

"Uh-huh."

"May I sit up?"

"Yeah."

She sat up cautiously, her hand still on the ground and still curled around the rock.

Now that she had a better look at the guy who stood over her, she saw that he was dressed like a hiker, wearing boots, rough pants and a plaid shirt. His hair, however, was cropped military-short and his face had the hard look of the guards she'd seen in the bunker.

Apparently, he was the only one of the security men in back of the cabin. The others were all closer to the building and in front where they hadn't seen anyone exit. It appeared that this guy hadn't seen Jonah.

Did he have a radio? Would he call for backup, or did he figure he could handle one lone woman on his own?

"How did you get out?" he demanded.

Seeing no point in lying, she said, "Through a hole in the floor."

"You mean there was an escape hatch."

"Yes."

She caught a flicker of movement and risked a quick glance behind the man. It was Jonah. She tried to keep her eyes off him, struggling not to give him away.

His gun was drawn. But if he fired it, the other guards would come running.

As Jonah crept closer, she moved the rock under her hand, getting ready to hit the guard in the leg.

Trying to buy Jonah a little time, she wavered where she sat, putting her other hand to her head. "I feel sick."

"Yeah, sure. Get up. We're going back to the front of the cabin."

"I can't."

He was about to give another order when something inside the cabin exploded. When his hand and head jerked up in surprise, she slammed the rock into his leg. He cried out, just as Jonah sprinted the last few yards to him and brought his gun down on the back of the man's head.

The guard slumped to the ground, but in the process, he squeezed the trigger of his gun, firing off a shot.

"Run for the tangle of brambles in back of me," Jonah ordered.

Without stopping to look back, she scrambled up and ran for the thicket. He was right in back of her. When they reached the tangle of underbrush, she spared a glance behind her to see another one of the guards running toward his fallen comrade.

Behind him the cabin was engulfed in flames that were shooting toward the trees, and she hoped they hadn't started a forest fire.

Jonah cursed under his breath and looked wildly around. The underbrush in this part of the forest wasn't thick enough to allow them to fade into the landscape.

"I hoped we could get away clean. Now we've got to put distance between us and them. Come on."

She didn't spare the breath to reply. Instead she took off after him, amazed that he could run so fast with his injured leg. Even though he'd been in the bunker for three weeks, he was in better shape than she was.

She was soon breathing hard and she had a stitch in her side, but she kept going.

After what seemed like miles, he stopped, and she saw he was trying to breathe quietly.

"What are you doing?" she puffed.

"Listening."

She did the same, but she heard no one behind them.

He allowed them a few minutes of rest, then said, "Come on."

They had started off again, when she picked up a noise somewhere above them.

"Down," Jonah ordered.

She got down, flattening herself under a tangle of brambles, the way he was doing.

"What's that?" she whispered.

"Helicopter."

"I guess it's not some random tourist flyby."

"No."

"Will they see us?"

"Don't know."

The noise grew louder, and she caught a glint of metal above the tops of the trees.

"Keep your face down." Jonah scooted away and she saw him gathering up handfuls of leaves. He threw them over her, then lay down beside her again and tossed more leaves over himself.

She could hear the helicopter getting closer and closer until it sounded like the spy in the sky was hovering above them. From the corner of her eye, she could see Jonah's hand gripping the SIG. She held her breath until the noise finally receded.

"We've got to get going while we can," Jonah told her.

"I know."

They both scrambled up, heading away from the burning cabin.

Once more, they heard the chopper coming back and once more they got down, digging into the leaves and waiting as the motor noise grew louder.

"If they didn't see me at the cabin, they may think I'm dead," Jonah muttered. "Unfortunately, when they start poking through the ashes, they won't find a body."

"I don't think the guy who caught me saw you."

"But he knows he was hit from behind."

When the noise receded, Jonah stood up and started jogging downhill.

They detoured around a large rock. "Lucky you looked out the window when you did," she said.

"I'm due for some luck."

Neither one of them was capable of moving quite as quickly now. "Did the fire trigger any memories?"

"You mean like when Mr. Luskin caught me and Teddy smoking out behind the garage?"

She laughed. "Teddy Luskin. I haven't thought about him in years."

"He came up with all kinds of ways to get into trouble. He was the guy who broke the gym windows."

"Did the fire trigger any memories from Afghanistan?"

His lips firmed. "Maybe."

"But you're not sure."

He balled his hands into fists at his sides. "I can see a house burning. But I don't know if it's anything real or if I'm making it up."

She knew she wasn't doing his nerves any good, and since right now their main job was to get away, she stopped trying to pry information out of him.

They kept moving at as fast a pace as she could manage. She wasn't sure how much territory they covered. She knew that Jonah's leg must be aching, but he didn't complain.

Ahead of her, she saw blue sky. Cautiously they peered through the screen of trees, and she spotted the black ribbon of a road.

"Could the guards come driving along here?"

"They could. I don't know where this road comes from or where it goes."

When a car passed, they ducked back into the trees.

"We've got to get out of here. Maybe we have to take a chance," Jonah muttered.

They could hear another vehicle approaching, something larger than a car.

"See if you can get us a ride," Jonah said.

"How?"

"Get out there and look charming."

She wasn't sure how to look charming, but she stepped to the side of the road and frantically waved her hand as a truck came around the curve.

At first she thought the driver wasn't going to stop, and she was getting ready to jump back into the woods when the truck slowed.

The driver rolled down the window and leaned toward her. "You need help, honey?"

He was a middle-aged man with thinning hair, broken veins all over his cheeks and nose, and what she'd call an honest face.

She started thinking fast. Yes, she was in trouble, but she wasn't going to tell him that she and Jonah had escaped from private security guards.

"Some crazy guys went after me and my boyfriend," she said, deliberately making her sentence ungrammatical. "We got to get away from them."

Jonah stepped out of the woods. "We'd surely appreciate a ride."

The driver eyed him, and she held her breath waiting to see if the offer of help extended to both of them.

"Sure. Hop in."

She exhaled, amazed that he didn't question their story. They both climbed into the cab, and the truck started off again.

"Name's Hank Keller," the driver said.

"Jim Baker," Jonah said without missing a beat.

"Like the preacher?"

Jonah laughed. "Yeah. They used to get me mixed up with him all the time." He gestured toward Sophia. "And this is Sara, my main squeeze."

She struggled to keep a straight face.

"So what happened to y'all?" the driver asked.

"We was camping," Jonah said, continuing the speech pattern

she had started. "And these guys came into our camp and started helping themselves to our stuff."

The driver jerked his head away from the road and Sophia had to clench her teeth to keep from telling him to watch where he was driving.

"You get hurt?"

"We was out fishin' at the time. We lit out and figured we'd come back for any gear that was left when it was safe."

The driver reached for the cell phone on the dashboard. "You want me to call the cops?"

Jonah pulled a long face. "Naw. Truth is, I had a beef with one of the guys. He reckons I owe him some money—and he reckons that gives him the right to rob us and kick us out of our own campsite."

"That's a plumb shame."

Jonah launched into an amusing tale about how he and Tommy had been best buddies until they'd had a misunderstanding.

Sophia kept her mouth shut, amazed at the way Jonah was spinning the tale out of whole cloth and at the way the truck driver was taking it all in.

"Where you headed?" he asked.

"Away from here."

"Y'all in trouble with the law?"

"Naw," Jonah allowed. "I got into some scrapes when I was a kid, but Sara keeps me honest now." He patted her on the knee.

The driver laughed. "Yeah. My old lady and me have the same arrangement."

Sophia kept silent while the men talked about beer and baseball and cars.

About fifty miles from where he'd picked them up, Hank brought the conversation back to their problem. "So they got all your money?"

"I have some hidden in my boot."

Sophia blinked, then remembered that Jonah had raided Montgomery's cash drawer.

A few miles farther on, Hank pulled into a gas station.

"This is close enough for us to walk home," Jonah said.

Hank got out, and she and Jonah did the same.

"Much obliged," he said, and the two men shook hands.

While the driver was inside paying for the gas, they turned down a side street and kept going.

"I can't believe the way you bonded with that guy," Sophia murmured. "Where did you pick up the gift of the gab?"

"Maybe I always had it."

"True. I do remember you could always tell a good story when it came time to collect homework."

They both laughed. She sobered as she looked around at the darkened road, suddenly conscious that they were in a rural area with no means of transportation. "What are we going to do for a car?"

Jonah kept his voice matter of fact. "I believe we're going to have to steal one."

"I was afraid you were going to say that."

"You have a better suggestion?"

"We can call the Light Street Detective Agency from a pay phone."

He stopped short. "I don't know anything about them, except what you've told me."

"They got me into the bunker. When we were in the cave, you asked what we were supposed to do when we got out. Doesn't that mean you were willing to ask for their help?"

"Maybe I was, but I'm thinking more clearly now. As far as I know, they have their own agenda."

"One of them got killed getting you out of there."

He had the grace to wince.

"Are you saying you have a different agenda?"

"Right. Now that I've got a name, I'm going to contact Colonel Luntz and find out what he knows about that briefing."

"Is that a good idea?"

"I guess I'll find out." He sat down on a fallen log and took off his boot. Reaching inside, he fished out the money he'd taken from Montgomery's office. After shuffling through the bills, he held them out to her.

"Maybe you'd better take this. You can call your friends and get them to pick you up."

"I'm not leaving you."

He tipped his head to the side. "And what if I say it's time to split up?"

## Chapter Fourteen

In the moonlight, Sophia turned to face him. She knew pride had something to do with the decisions he was making. He'd been held in hostile captivity, then rescued by her and Phil. Now he needed to prove that he was in charge of his own destiny. Yet she wasn't going to let him shove her out of the picture.

"You are not going to walk away from me. Not after…" She had been about to say, "not after making love with me and getting my hopes up." Instead she switched the comment. "Not after what we've been through together."

She saw his jaw tighten.

"What are you thinking?" she demanded. "That I'm a spy? That Montgomery sent me along with you to make sure I get the information?"

"No," he allowed.

"Well, that's something."

"I know you risked a lot to get me out of there. I know a man got killed in the process. But I don't know what's going to happen when I find Colonel Luntz."

"Which is a good reason for me to stay with you."

"It could be dangerous."

"No more dangerous than what happened in the cave. Or

almost getting burned up in that cabin. Or my getting caught by that guard."

When he answered with a tight nod, she swallowed hard and managed to ask, "If you had your choice, would you want me with you or not?"

Her chest was so tight that she could hardly breathe as she waited for the answer.

"With me," he finally said.

"Good," she managed to say. It was a mild representation of what she was feeling.

She wanted to reach for him and pull him close. She needed that contact, needed to feel him respond to her. But she forced herself to stay where she was.

"Let's find some transportation," she suggested.

"I doubt that you're going to charm anyone out of a car."

"Right."

He kept his gaze fixed on her face. "I'm planning to fall back on the skills I learned in high school. You still have the opportunity to opt out of this expedition, you know."

"No." She stood. "Let's get it over with."

She fell back a pace, watching Jonah walk. The leg had to be paining him, but he wasn't complaining. That was the kind of man he was—and the kind of boy he'd been. His life had been a lot tougher than she'd imagined. Too bad she hadn't known back then that he'd put up such a tough-guy front. But what would she have done about it? She'd just been rich little Sophia Rhodes—not Dr. Sophia Rhodes with the professional training to give her insights into Jonah Baker's character.

The moon provided some light as they walked down the road, passing rural mailboxes. Jonah chose a darkened lane and started up it. The house at the top of a hill wasn't a very impressive residence. From what she could see, it looked like a small box with a gabled room and a front stoop that was listing to one side.

Below the house, several cars were parked. Jonah studied the collection, then walked to one that looked as though it had been in a couple of minor accidents. The back bumper was caved in and the right front wheel barely cleared one of the fenders.

"Nobody's gonna miss this thing," he muttered. "If it will start." He looked at her. "Keep watch."

He handed her the gun.

"You don't want me to shoot anyone, do you?" she asked, hearing the quaver in her voice.

"Use your judgment."

He tried the front door of the vehicle and found it open. A good sign, she supposed. Nobody cared enough to lock it up.

Slipping inside, he wedged himself onto the floor below the steering wheel and began fiddling with wires.

She watched nervously, expecting someone to discover what they were doing and come charging out of the house with a shotgun. She was thankful when nobody appeared.

When the car started, Jonah eased up from his position on the floor. But as she hurried around to the passenger door, a light came on in the house.

Trouble!

"Hold it right there," a voice boomed out.

She almost jumped out of her skin, then jumped again as a blast from the shotgun she'd pictured earlier split the air.

Lucky for her, the guy was too far away to do any serious damage.

"Get in," Jonah shouted.

She jumped into the car and slammed the door as he headed down the hill.

The engine sputtered, and he cursed. Behind them, another blast sounded.

She cringed down in the seat. "I guess he'd rather get us than save his car."

"Better fire a couple of shots across his bow."

"Are you crazy?"

As Jonah kept driving, he reached over and took the gun from her, then leaned out the window and got off several shots.

"Stop."

"I'm not trying to hit him, just scare him."

"Great."

She had been looking behind her. When she swiveled to the front again, she gasped. "Jonah, watch out."

He brought his attention to the road again, then yanked the wheel hard, barely missing a fence post.

She breathed out a sigh, then looked behind them again. "The good news is that he's stopped."

"The bad news is that he may call the cops. And we don't want to get nailed for armed robbery."

She winced.

Jonah kept going, picking up speed as he barreled onto the road and turned right.

"You know where we're going?"

"I wish I did."

He drove for another few miles, then pulled into another darkened lane.

"Now what?"

"We have to change the license plates."

"How do we do that?"

"Borrow some. Stay here."

He got out and cut the engine, then opened the trunk and

rummaged inside. He must have found what he was looking for because he went to work on the plates.

When they were off the front and rear of the car, he trotted up the hill and disappeared.

She sat rigidly in her seat, waiting to hear gunfire again.

Finally, Jonah came limping back down the hill and held up a set of plates for her to see. Then he replaced the ones that had been on the car.

When he climbed back inside, he sat for a minute with his head thrown back against the headrest.

She reached over and laid her palm atop his right hand where it rested on the steering wheel.

"Your leg is hurting." She didn't wait for affirmation. "Let me drive."

His head turned toward her. "You're sure you want to drive a stolen car?"

"What's the difference between driving and being a passenger?"

"Not much, I guess."

He twisted the wires together to start the engine again, then pulled up the emergency brake while they switched places.

She accelerated slowly, getting the feel of the vehicle as she headed down the highway.

When she came to a sign that pointed to Blackwater Falls and Morgantown, she started to ask Jonah which way to go. But he had fallen asleep.

She decided to head northeast, toward a more populated area.

When she found herself getting sleepy, she started looking for a place to spend the night. She pulled into a one-story, inexpensive motor court and laid her hand on Jonah's shoulder.

He came awake with a jerk, pointing the gun toward her.

"Jonah!"

He focused on her and lowered the weapon. "Sorry. I told you I was dangerous."

"No, you're not. I just startled you."

"Stop denying the obvious."

"That was your army combat instincts kicking in."

"Is that your professional opinion?"

"Yes. And I'm too tired to argue. I just want to get us a room."

"How far are we from where Hank let us off?"

"Seventy-five miles."

"I hope that's good enough."

"You think they're going to check every little motel between here and D.C.?"

"If they're desperate enough. Is that where we're headed?"

"In that general direction. I figured we'd be better off in an urban area."

His expression sharpened. "You're not taking me to your friends in Baltimore, are you?"

She sighed. "Not unless you want to go there."

"I don't!"

She wanted to tell him he was being stubborn, but she knew that wouldn't help the situation. Instead, she asked for some of the cash so she could pay for the night.

"Tell them you want a room in back where it's quiet."

He gave her all of the money, and she paid cash, then climbed in again and drove to the other side of the building. The room wasn't palatial but it was clean.

She wanted to talk to Jonah, but he was making it clear that he wasn't much interested in communication. Instead she used the facilities and took a quick shower, then turned the bathroom over to him.

Wishing she had a change of clothes, she climbed into bed in her underwear, then listened to the shower running. He stayed under the water for a long time, and when he opened the bathroom door, she could see him in the light coming in around the edges of the curtains.

Wearing only his briefs, he slipped into the other side of the bed, and she lay for a minute, listening to the sound of his breathing.

When she couldn't stand it any longer, she closed the distance between them and turned on her side, reaching for him and snuggling close.

She could feel his instant tension.

"Don't put barriers between us," she said.

"I have to."

It was hard to speak around the constriction in her throat. "Is that a moral imperative or a personal decision about us?"

"Both."

She cradled her head against his shoulder. "Maybe you can explain your thinking."

He dragged in a breath and let it out. "I have a big fat hole in my memory. I don't know what's true and what isn't. I don't know what happened in Afghanistan, but I'm pretty sure it's something bad. And if that's not enough, when you tried to dig into it, I attacked you."

"We'll fix all that," she murmured.

"How can you be sure?"

"Because of your determination," she answered. "You *want* to fix it, badly, so you *will*."

"Are you telling me every nut case who *wants* to get well does?"

"You're not a nut case. Montgomery screwed with your mind."

"What's the difference?"

"A lot." She sighed. "Look, right now, you need to relax."

"Easier said than done," he muttered.

"Turn over. Let me massage your back and shoulder muscles."

He hesitated for a moment, then rolled to his stomach.

"There's some hand cream in the bathroom." She went to get it, then pulled down the covers.

He was lying with his eyes closed, his arms folded under his head. She poured some of the slippery white liquid into her hands, then straddled his body at his waist. She leaned over him and started massaging the tense muscles of his neck and shoulders and back.

After a moment, he gave a deep sigh of pleasure, and she kept working on him with slick hands, trying not to notice that straddling him and touching him was turning her on. Her breasts started to feel full and achy, and she couldn't stop herself from pressing her sex downward to increase her own pleasure.

Partly to distract herself, she began talking to him in a low voice.

"Where was the briefing with Luntz?"

"Beltsville, Maryland."

"Ah, so you came up with the location."

He sounded surprised. "Yeah. I didn't remember it before. But I guess it popped back into my head."

"That's good. Why there?" she asked, trying to focus on business and not the heat rushing through her body.

"They used some abandoned buildings on the campus at the Agricultural Research Center."

She sat up straighter. "Was Montgomery there?"

"I don't think so."

"Just Luntz and the group going on the mission?"

"Yes."

"How long were you in Afghanistan?"

"Eighteen hours," he answered. "Then it all blew up in our faces."

She wanted to ask how, but she didn't push in that direction.

"Was Luntz with you in Afghanistan?" she asked instead.

"No."

"Do you know the real mission?"

"No."

She had felt his tension coming back as she asked the last few questions.

"Sorry," she murmured.

"You got some stuff out of me," he said in a gritty voice.

"I should stop being so aggressive."

"Or maybe you shouldn't." He laughed. "I know what you're doing. And I don't mean your questions. I can feel the heat coming off you."

He slowly rolled under her, giving her time to adjust to the changed position. When he came to rest on his back, she realized that she wasn't the only one who had been turned on by her slippery hands moving over him.

She made a strangled sound as she felt him pressing against her. When he reached up to pull her down to his chest, she came willingly.

She had thought he was trying to stay away from her. Apparently it hadn't worked.

Reaching around her, he unhooked her bra, and she pulled it out of the way and tossed it to the other side of the bed. Then he pulled her down, kneading her back the way she had done his.

Her breasts swayed against his chest, making her crave more. She raised up only enough to pull her panties off one leg, leaving them clinging to the other. Then she did the same with him, pulling down his briefs far enough so that she had full access to him.

She was already swollen and slick, and she rubbed herself against him, loving his wonderful hardness and heat.

He made a strangled exclamation as she drove them both wild with need. Then she brought him inside her.

Her eyes locked with his, and she stayed where she was

without moving for half a minute, teasing them both almost beyond endurance.

He was the one who forced the issue, raising his hips and pressing farther into her.

She cried out and began to move, because that was her only option.

"I want to see you play with your breasts," he said, his voice thick.

She did as he asked, boldly lifting her breasts toward him, then plucking and twisting at the tips because it gave them both pleasure.

It was wonderful to move in this dance of sexual fulfillment with him. Wonderful to see his face and so much of his body as she moved above him.

She pulled back as far as she could and still remain joined to him, then she looked down at the place where their bodies merged, marveling at the way that intimate connection looked.

She watched him follow her gaze, his face molten with heat.

With an exclamation of pure joy, she plunged down again, driving them both to the brink.

Her movements became wilder. Less controlled. She pushed them both to a high peak of pleasure, then tumbled over the edge, taking him with her in a rush of deep fulfillment.

Breathing hard, she collapsed on top of him, wrapping her arms around him and holding him tight.

"I love you," she whispered.

She heard his sharp indrawn breath.

"No."

"I think a while ago you advised me not to tell you what you feel. Give me the same courtesy."

"You don't want to get mixed up with me."

"Like I said, let me be the judge of that."

Sitting up was too much work, so she bent forward, clasping

his sweat- and lotion-slick body as she stretched out on top of him, keeping him inside her.

She longed to hear him say the same thing she had said. But she knew he wasn't going to do it. Not until he had dealt with the memory problem.

Or maybe never, if he let his stubborn pride rule his emotions. In the vulnerable recesses of her heart, she understood that she had to be prepared for that, too.

# Chapter Fifteen

Jonah found a house where the people were obviously on an extended trip and traded in the old clunker for a newer model. The trade involved breaking into the house and taking a spare set of keys. He wasn't enjoying all the illegal activity, but he made himself feel better about it by keeping a list of people he had to reimburse.

As they headed toward Washington, D.C., he pulled into a fast-food restaurant and got in line for the take-out window.

They were using the money from Montgomery's office as sparingly as possible, but they were going to need an infusion of cash if they didn't change their fugitive status soon.

He and Sophia each ordered burgers, french fries and sodas. As they sat in the car eating, he slid her a sidewise glance. Since the first car heist, she hadn't complained about his problem-solving solutions, even though he was sure she didn't like being on the wrong side of the law.

She dipped a french fry in ketchup. "I have a suggestion for how to approach Luntz."

"Why do I think I'm not going to like it?"

"Because you don't trust my judgment."

He felt a pang of regret. "That's not true."

"Then at least listen to my plan."

He took a bite of his burger and leaned back against the seat. "Okay."

When she began to talk, he knew his suspicions had been right. He didn't like what he was hearing. Unfortunately, her scheme made sense. But he told her they were going to look for every flaw they could find in her logic before they put it into action.

Since he couldn't dredge up any objections, they checked out Luntz's house. He lived in Potomac, Maryland, in what had once been prime horse country. In recent years, many of the horse farms had been turned into McMansion subdivisions. There were still some old estates where the owners had kept the property intact. Colonel Luntz's was one of them.

Jonah drove past the entrance several times. The approach to the house was up a curving driveway, screened by trees. He didn't know what was going on up there. And he needed to find out.

Next they stopped at a mall and bought some equipment, including two prepaid cell phones, and a directional mike so he could pick up conversations at a distance.

"That's about it for our money," he said as they headed toward the colonel's house.

Sophia nodded.

"Maybe I could play guitar outside the mall and collect tips."

"Do you know how to play?"

"Yeah," he answered. "I learned at Fort Benning. I used to amuse my friends with raunchy ballads."

She laughed. "I'd like to hear them."

"But then I'd have to steal a guitar—which would defeat the purpose of the exercise."

She laughed again as they turned down the road where Luntz lived.

Jonah drove past and turned off into a patch of woods. Then

he got out and started back to the estate on foot while Sophia waited in the car.

Once he'd slipped under a split rail fence from the neighboring property, he waited and listened for signs that the place was being guarded.

He heard only the rustling of small animals in the underbrush.

Staying low and slipping through the woods, he came out into a well-kept garden, surrounding a redbrick Georgian two-story house.

As he approached the structure, he could see lights on inside. A gray-haired man in casual clothes was sitting in a den watching news on television. He looked to be in his fifties, and Jonah felt a spark of recognition. As he stared at the man's face, he tried to come up with more details of the briefing.

He could picture Luntz standing at the front of a room full of troops. But that was all. None of what the guy had been saying was coming through.

Jonah clenched his fists, then ordered himself to stop trying to force memories. It didn't do any good. They came back when they were good and ready—or not at all.

What he had to do was focus on the present assignment—determining that it was safe enough for Sophia to come calling on the man inside the house.

He strained his ears. As far as he could tell, there was no sound coming from the interior except the television.

As he circled the property, he noted the exterior features and looked in other windows, but he saw no one else. When he checked the detached garage, he found two cars.

It was almost too perfect, with Luntz at home alone and watching television.

Was this a setup? Or was the man entirely comfortable in his own surroundings and sure that he wasn't in any kind of trouble?

Slipping back into the woods, Jonah called Sophia on the cell phone.

"Give me ten minutes. Then come on ahead."

"Okay."

He hung up, then hurried back to the house, where he secured his pack on his back, then climbed up a drainpipe to the top of the covered patio. From there he crossed to an upstairs window and carefully cut a circle in one of the panes with a glass cutter. Then he slipped inside and tiptoed toward the stairs.

He tried to stay calm, but his stomach was tied in knots.

Stationing himself in the shadows of the hall, he waited for the doorbell to ring.

It did—on schedule.

Moments later, he heard footsteps on the stone floor of the lower hall. Then Luntz turned on the exterior light and opened the door.

"May I help you?" he asked.

From the top of the stairs, Jonah could hear Sophia's voice drifting through the doorway. "I'm sorry to bother you so late in the evening."

"Yes?" Luntz said.

"I'm Sara Rollins," she said, giving the name they'd agreed upon. "I'm a clinical psychologist, and I've been working with a patient named Jonah Baker. He's mentioned you several times in our sessions, and I'm hoping you can give me some information about him."

"Come in."

She did, and he closed the door behind her.

"Where is Baker?"

"I'm not at liberty to say."

"Why not?"

"He's at a secure government facility."

"Because?"

"He apparently had some kind of breakdown on an assignment in Afghanistan. And I understand that you set up the mission."

"Where did you get that information?" Luntz asked sharply.

"I was able to hypnotize Baker."

"Interesting."

"I'm not making much progress with him, and I was hoping you could give me some useful information about him."

He gestured toward the back of the house. "Why didn't you call me?"

"I was afraid you wouldn't see me if I did. I was hoping that if I just came here, you wouldn't turn me away."

"Why don't we sit down?"

"Thank you."

She started down the hall, and Jonah had started to walk down the steps when two more men came out of another doorway and moved quickly up on either side of Sophia, grabbing her arms.

Sophia cried out as they hustled her toward the room where Luntz had been sitting like a goddamn decoy, pretending he was totally alone.

Jonah knew that now. He also knew something else. Luntz wasn't an innocent bystander. He was up to his eyeballs in this, and he'd been prepared for trouble.

Jonah didn't recognize either of the men who had grabbed Sophia, but they looked like they'd been cut from the same mold as the security guards in the bunker.

Were there other guards in the house?

And how was he going to get Sophia out of here?

Cursing his own stupidity for letting her put herself in danger, Jonah tiptoed back up the main staircase. He'd thought it was safe for Sophia to come in here. Now he knew how wrong he was.

With his heart pounding, he looked back over his shoulder.

He'd seen another set of stairs which led to the back of the house. Maybe that was his best bet.

Scrambling for a plan, he pulled out his SIG and hurried to the alternate stairway, then quickly descended. At the bottom he paused to make sure he was alone. No other men had materialized, but that didn't mean they weren't here.

He flattened himself against the wall and moved down the hall toward the family room. Through the doorway he saw that they had pushed Sophia into a chair and were grouped around her.

"He sent you," Luntz growled.

"No."

One of the men answered. "She was at the bunker. And she sure as hell wasn't part of the team there."

"Shut up," Luntz growled. "We're asking questions, not giving out information."

The man clamped his mouth shut.

"Where is he?" Luntz demanded.

She raised her chin. "I don't know."

"I don't believe you." For emphasis, he pulled back his hand, then slapped her across the face.

She made a startled sound.

"You're going to tell us."

When he saw Luntz strike her, Jonah's anger flared. Yet he knew that if he let emotions rule him, they were both going to end up dead.

"Where is he?" Luntz asked again, his voice menacing. "It will be easier on you if you tell me."

Jonah pulled the phone from his pocket and called Luntz's number.

As it rang, all of the men focused on the sound.

Jonah dashed forward and hit one of them on the back of the head with the gun. He went down, but when Jonah struck at the other guy, he had already moved.

From the corner of his eye, he saw Sophia lash out at Luntz, her foot catching him square in the crotch. He doubled over, groaning.

But Jonah had his own problems. The other guard was trying to pull his gun out of the holster on his belt so he could get off a shot.

Jonah chopped at the guard's gun hand, and the man cried out. But that didn't stop him from springing forward.

Sophia backed up a step and swung her purse by the strap, hitting him on the back of the neck. It was enough of a distraction for Jonah to come up with a fist to the man's chin.

He went down, joining his partner on the floor.

It had all happened in a matter of seconds. The uniformed men both lay unconscious at his feet. Luntz was still doubled over.

Jonah ripped the cord off a lamp, pushed Luntz into the chair and handed Sophia the gun.

"Cover him," he said as he tied the man's hands behind his back.

When he'd secured the colonel, he gave him a narrow-eyed look. "What the hell is going on?"

"You won't get that information from me."

"We'll see about that."

"If I were you, I'd get out of here. Reinforcements are on the way."

"Why am I the key to your Afghanistan plot?"

The colonel lifted his chin. "Who says there's a plot, and who says you're the key? You're giving yourself too much credit."

"Oh, come on. You had me locked up in an underground bunker to get information out of me."

"Not me. Montgomery."

"So you know him."

Realizing he'd made a mistake, the man paled. But his voice remained firm. "I repeat, you'd better get out while the getting is good."

One of the guards groaned and started to roll over. Jonah gave him a kick in the head with his boot, and the guy went quiet again.

Sophia winced. "We should leave."

"She's right," Luntz confirmed.

Sophia put a hand on Jonah's arm. "I think we'd better split. He's not going to tell us anything."

"I wouldn't bet on it."

As Luntz had done to Sophia, Jonah swung back his arm, then delivered a flat-hand blow to the man's mouth.

He gasped, and when he opened his mouth again, it was bloody. He glared at Jonah. "How dare you."

Jonah felt his blood surge. He had been angry and frustrated for a long time, and finally he had an outlet for that anger. "There's a lot more where that came from. Who's running the show? You or Montgomery?"

The colonel pressed his lips together.

"I can find out who was authorized to use that bunker," he said, wondering if that was really true.

He was pleased to get a reaction out of the man.

"I'll bet you didn't know there was a back way in."

Luntz's face showed that the guess had been right.

"Too bad you couldn't control access," he taunted. He wanted to strip off the guy's clothing, tie him down on a bed and make him think he was going to end up with his balls handed to him on a platter. But not with Sophia watching. Maybe it was good that she was here, because that would keep him from stepping over a line that he could never come back across.

Outside, Jonah heard a car door slam.

Luntz gave him a triumphant look.

Jonah turned to Sophia. "Come on."

He hurried out of the room, and she followed. In the doorway he reached into his pack, then tossed two tear gas canisters inside.

As the room filled with gas, Luntz began to cough, and Jonah guided Sophia out the back door and around the side of the house.

Inside he could hear shouts, coughing and cursing.

"You're driving. Get in the car."

Sophia got into the driver's seat while Jonah turned and shot out all four tires of the SUV that had pulled up in the driveway. Someone came running out the front door, shooting.

Jonah ducked into the passenger seat and slammed the door as Sophia took off down the driveway. Careening through the decorative brick posts, she headed for the route that they'd agreed on earlier in case they had to make a quick getaway.


THEY DROVE for several miles.

"Now what?" Sophia asked.

"I don't know."

She cleared her throat. "Would you consider calling the Light Street Detective Agency?"

"I don't want to."

"I know. But we're out of options and out of money."

He sighed, finally conceding the point. "Yeah."

She pulled the phone out of her purse, put it on speaker phone and pressed in a number. Someone answered on the first ring.

"This is Sophia Rhodes."

"Thank God," a woman answered. "This is Kathryn Kelley."

Jonah remembered she was the woman who had recruited Sophia for this assignment.

"Where are you?" Kelley asked.

"In Potomac, Maryland."

"You, Phil and Baker?"

She sucked in a breath. "Phil didn't make it. But I have Jonah Baker with me."

"You want us to pick you up?"

She glanced at Jonah.

"Yes," he answered.

"Okay. Give me a moment." They waited without speaking for Kelley to return. When she came back on the line, she said, "Take Route 108 across Montgomery and Howard counties. Do you know how to get there?"

"Yes."

"Turn off on New Hampshire Avenue, then right onto Brighton Dam Road and head for Brighton Dam Park. We'll meet you in the parking lot across the highway from the park. Do you know where that is?"

Jonah had no idea, but Sophia answered, "Yes."

When she hung up, Jonah slumped in his seat, and Sophia reached out to touch his knee.

His leg twitched. "That didn't work out so well."

"Sorry. I guess it wasn't such a great idea."

"I shouldn't have let you risk it. I'm obviously not functioning at top efficiency."

"Stop blaming yourself."

"He hurt you."

"It was only one slap."

"That was enough."

"I'm tougher than I look."

"I know."

"Thanks for that, at least."

"What's that supposed to mean?"

She huffed out a breath. "You're trying to distance yourself from me."

"For your own good."

She turned her head toward him. "You have to let me be the judge of that."

"I'm not used to answering to anyone besides myself. Well, at least when I'm not following orders."

"That's obvious."

He wasn't sure how to respond, so he pressed his lips together, waiting for her to demand some answer that he wasn't ready to give.

Maybe he never would be.

To his relief, it seemed that Sophia had decided not to keep pressing him.

They traveled in silence until she said, "Here's the turnoff."

They rode past woods, then came to a parking area on their right. In the moonlight, he could see the ground sloping along the side of a dam into what looked like a black chasm.

"What's down there?"

"Picnic tables. Playground equipment. A stream where the water spills off from the dam."

"It's relatively open?"

"Yes."

"What about the other side?" he asked, looking to his left where he saw a wooded area with water sparkling in the moonlight. "Is that a lake?"

"That's a reservoir, with a naturalized park along the shore. It's full of huge azaleas planted all through the woods. Right now, they're blooming. In the daylight, it's like a fairyland with big splashes of color."

He stared into the woods. Some of the flowers must be white because they stood out in the moonlight.

"There are trails with blooming bushes towering over your head on either side. I tell people that if they live around here and don't visit in the spring, they're crazy." She laughed. "And here we are. Perfect timing! Too bad we can't see much in the dark."

"Yeah."

In his life, he hadn't given himself much time to stop and smell the flowers. He didn't even know if azaleas had much scent.

Climbing out of the car, he was glad to stretch his cramped muscles. He'd been doing too much walking on the damn leg. He was just leaning down to massage it when a noise made him stop short.

Sophia came around to his side, her look questioning. "What?"

He swore, listening for another moment to be sure. Unfortunately, the noise was all too familiar. "Another helicopter coming this way."

"You think?"

He took a quick look at their surroundings, wondering if the moonlight was a help or not. It gave him some additional night vision, but that was also true for the enemy.

The open area below the dam was deep in shadow now. But a searchlight would illuminate anyone down there like roaches running for cover when you turned on the kitchen light in the middle of the night.

He swung the other way, seeing the trees and flower-covered bushes along the lake.

That was their better bet.

"Into the woods. Hurry."

## Chapter Sixteen

Headlights knifed down the road, setting Jonah's heart pounding. Were more guards on the way?

He held his breath until the car sped past. Grabbing Sophia's hand he led her across the four-lane highway. She took the lead, running down a wide path lined with huge bushes that towered over them.

After twenty yards, she veered off onto a narrow track leading uphill between eight-foot tall azaleas. When she found a small opening, she plunged under the foliage on the left, wedging herself in and making room for Jonah.

"How did they figure out we came here?" she whispered as they curled around each other.

He made an angry sound. "Unfortunately, it looks like they put a transponder on the car."

"Like I used to track you around the bunker?"

"Yes."

He looked out, wishing he'd driven the car over the side of the parking area before they'd crossed the road. It would have plunged down into the stream valley below the dam, and the bad guys might have thought that he and Sophia had gone over the edge with it. But it was too late for that now. The helicopter was almost above them.

In fact he could hear two choppers. One right here and the other a little farther away.

Across the road, he could see lights moving back and forth, confirming his assumption about the transponder. The bad guys were starting with the car. When they realized it was empty, they'd widen their search.

As he expected, the helicopter began to circle, the light striking the bushes, making sudden splashes of color leap out of the blackness as the wind from the rotors whipped the branches, sending blossoms swirling into the air.

He brought his mouth to Sophia's ear. "Don't move."

Reaching for his SIG, he worked his hand into firing position as he wrapped his free arm around her and pressed his lips to her cheek.

The spotlight wove through the wooded area, still illuminating the blooming bushes, still tearing the blossoms off their stems. On its first pass, it missed them. Then it swung back, and he tensed, waiting for the light to strike their hiding place.

When it did, he stopped breathing.

The machine hovered, and he was pretty sure the spotters had found them.

He brought his mouth to Sophia's ear. "Stay under the bushes, but see how far you can get from this spot. If you can make it to the reservoir without being seen, maybe you can swim across and get away."

She turned her head. "What about you?"

"They can't land in the trees. They have to use the open space in the parking lot. I'm going to take out as many of them as I can."

Before she could object, he left her, wiggling through the bushes and slithering out. Climbing to his feet, he started running back up the trail toward the road.

He reached the fence that marked the edge of the wooded area as the helicopter zoomed toward the parking lot. It was still a hundred feet in the air when the rotors choked and sputtered, and the machine came crashing down to the blacktop—where it burst into flames.

Jonah leaped back, his gun at the ready.

In the light from the burning machine, a shape materialized out of the darkness, something rushing at him so fast that he couldn't see anything but a blur of motion. Then hands with super-human strength grabbed him, lifting the gun from his grasp before he could fire.

"Sophia?" another voice called. "Are you there? Are you all right? Come out. It's Hunter Kelley, from Light Street."

"Here. I'm here." Sophia came running up the path, her eyes wide.

The man who was holding Jonah let go, and he stepped quickly back.

Sophia ran to Jonah. "Are you all right?" she asked.

"Yes." Before he could say anything further, more figures materialized out of the darkness, and he stared at the group gathering around him. They were all tough-looking men, but different in some fundamental way from the guards at the bunker.

"What did you do to the chopper?" he asked.

The one named Hunter Kelley answered. "We thought they might try something like this, so we brought a device that jammed the rotor."

He stared at the guy, taking in the words but not crediting them. "That would be very convenient for terrorists. But as far as I know, it's not possible."

"Our technology is beyond current state of the art. The jamming device isn't something we've made public or that we use very often. But this is one of those times. When the authorities investigate, it will look like a mechanical failure."

Stunned, Jonah stared at him. "And when the cops find a

chopper full of tough guys here, what are they going to think was going on?"

"Hell if I know," the man who had grabbed Jonah's gun answered. "But we'd better split. By the way, my name is Nicholas Vickers."

"Nice to meet you," he said, wondering how the guy had moved so fast.

"Likewise."

He led them down the stretch of highway to the other side of the dam, where another chopper had landed.

In the distance, they could hear the sound of fire engines.

"Better hurry," Vickers said.

They all climbed into the helicopter and strapped in. As soon as they were secured in place, the machine took off. From the air, Jonah got a quick look at the burning machine before they flew away.

Sophia sat next to Jonah, holding his hand tightly.

He squeezed her fingers, glad that it was almost impossible to talk above the noise.

Though he expected to see the lights of Baltimore ahead of them, they were heading toward a sparsely populated area. About an hour later, they landed in a clearing beside a long, low building in the middle of a pine forest.

When they had exited and were far enough away from the rotor to talk, he asked, "Where are we?"

"The Randolph Security research facility in western Maryland," Hunter Kelley answered.

They walked into a spacious front hall.

"We were in kind of a rush to get away, so I didn't get to introduce myself," the man who had been piloting the helicopter said. "I'm Jed Prentiss."

The others also offered names.

"Max Dakota."

"Cameron Randolph."

"And Thorn Devereaux."

Two women came down the hall, one of them a redhead and one a blond.

"I'm Kathryn Kelley, Hunter's wife," the redhead said, moving to her husband's side.

"And I'm Jo O'Malley, head of the Light Street Detective Agency. Cam's wife and partner."

"Glad to meet you all," Jonah said, trying to relax. Though he didn't know these people and had been afraid to trust them, so far, things were going surprisingly well.

"I'm afraid I'm the one who got Sophia into this," Kathryn Kelley said.

"I'm glad you did," Sophia answered.

Jonah gave her a long look. "You almost got killed a time or two."

She swallowed. "What's important is that we got you out of the bunker."

"But not your friend Phil," Jonah reminded him.

Cameron Randolph gave him a grave look. "We're all mourning him. He wasn't with our organization long, but we knew he was a good man. However, there's something he didn't want us to tell Sophia before they left for the cavern. He had inoperable cancer."

"What?" Sophia gasped.

"That's why he volunteered for the mission. He didn't have long to live and he was prepared to go out with his boots on—if that's what it took to get you out of there."

Jonah tried to cope with the shock of this new knowledge. "So that was why he was so insistent on holding off the guards while we went down the tunnel."

"That sounds right."

Kathryn turned to Sophia. "I'm sorry we kept you in the dark about his condition. He wouldn't let us tell you. He was afraid you wouldn't go with him if you thought he was unreliable."

She opened her mouth then closed it again, obviously reevaluating everything she'd known about the man.

"I was starting to think he was a drug addict," she whispered.

Randolph nodded, then said, "After what you've been through, you need some R and R. Let's start with food. Then sleep."

The thought of food and sleep made Jonah realize how hungry and tired he was.

"We've got a spread set out down the hall."

They kept walking and came to a comfortable lounge with sofas, chairs and tables. Plates and dishes of food were spread out on a long sideboard at the back of the room.

Jonah wandered over and looked at the selections, which included steak, baked potatoes with all the trimmings, roast turkey with gravy, stuffing and cranberry sauce and candied sweet potatoes.

"How did you get all this together on short notice?"

"We've been waiting for you to arrive," Jo O'Malley said. "And we wanted to make it a festive meal."

"Well, thanks."

Everybody helped themselves to food. Jonah opted for the turkey and trimmings, thinking how much it was like the Thanksgiving meals he'd seen on television—and better than anything his mom had been able to scrape together.

He brought his food to a sofa and leaned back with the plate on his lap.

Sophia sat beside him.

"You okay?" she asked.

"Yeah," he answered automatically as he ate and watched how the other men and women interacted. They had obviously been together for a long time, and they were all perfectly comfortable with each other.

All of them were eating, except the guy named Nick Vickers. He'd gotten a bottle of something red out of the refrigerator under the sideboard and was sipping slowly. From here, it looked like blood. What was he? One of those Goths who thought they were vampires?"

He felt a chill travel over his skin as he remembered the scene at the dam, when Vickers had moved through the night with super-human speed.

From across the room, Vickers smiled at him, and he got the feeling that the guy knew exactly what he was thinking.

He dragged his gaze away from Vickers and looked at the others again, enjoying the meal and talking in quiet voices.

He could dimly remember a time like that—when he'd been close to the guys in his unit. But that seemed like a dream that he only half remembered.

Cameron Randolph was looking at him. "So, why were they holding you in the bunker?" he asked.

"That's a pretty direct question," Jonah countered.

"We want to find out how much you understand about the situation."

Well, here it was. He was going to explain what a mess he was. He took a sip of the soda he'd gotten from the sideboard, then he told them about the memories of Thailand and about Afghanistan and about the nightmares.

As he spoke, he could feel sweat trickling down the back of his neck.

"I think you held up better than most people would have," Randolph said.

"Why do you think so?" Jonah challenged.

"Because you made it here."

"With Sophia's help. I couldn't have done it without her—and Phil."

"Yes. They played a very important role."

"Jonah and I made a good team," she murmured.

Randolph turned back to Jonah. "And don't minimize your achievements. You gave us a very coherent account of the past few weeks."

He hadn't thought of it that way.

Sophia covered his hand with hers and squeezed. "See? That's what I've been telling you," she murmured.

He wasn't sure what he would have said if he'd been alone with her, but Thorn Devereaux broke in to the exchange.

Clearing his throat, he said, "I sense that you're impatient to get to work."

"If you mean getting my memories back, then you're right."

"We have something that may help you, something we've tried with other people who had chunks of their past missing."

Jonah sat up straighter, all his attention focused on the man.

"You know that electroshock therapy often makes people lose their memories?"

He nodded.

"I've invented a machine that reverses the process. We've used it with success on a woman who came here from the future on a secret mission."

Jonah blinked. "A woman who came from the future? You're kidding, right?"

"No," Max Dakota answered. "She's my wife, Annie. She was sent here to prevent an event that set the world on a course with disaster. Only, when she got here, she didn't remember her mission."

Jonah glanced at Sophia and saw that she looked as thunderstruck as he.

"It sounds fantastic, but it's the truth. She's not here now because she's pregnant with our first child."

"Congratulations," Sophia said.

"Did it work?" Jonah asked. "I mean—the treatment."

"Yeah. But there's some risk involved," Devereaux answered.

"What risks?" Jonah demanded.

"If we bring back your memories from Afghanistan, you could forget everything you've learned since."

He nodded, considering that possibility.

"And there's some risk of brain injury."

"Then we won't do it!" Sophia said, her voice high and strained.

"Yeah, we will," Jonah answered, because he knew that he had to recover his past. No matter what.

"We should discuss this," Sophia said.

"No. I'm tired of being at the mercy of men like Luntz and Montgomery."

"For what it's worth, we think Montgomery is working for Luntz," Jed Prentiss said.

"Why didn't you tell me that?" Sophia snapped.

"We didn't know until after you left. We tried to communicate the information to Phil, but we couldn't get through to the cave."

"Yes, I remember his trying to contact you," she murmured.

Jonah stood. "Let's go zap my brain."

Sophia gave him a dark look, but she also stood.

"It would be better if you got some sleep first," Thorn said, and Sophia agreed.

Jonah looked at her, seeing the anxious expression on her face. Obviously she was hoping for the chance to talk him out of it.

"Maybe," he answered both her and Thorn. "But I'm not going to be able to sleep until we get this done. So let's get the show on the road."

Thorn stood and led the way down the hall to a wing of the building that looked like an outpatient clinic. They passed various rooms with medical equipment and ended up in what might have been a doctor's consultation room. Thorn sat down behind the desk, and Jonah and Sophia took the guest chairs. He wanted to tell her to leave now and let him handle this, but he was pretty sure she would ignore the request. And maybe she did have the right to stay, because he wouldn't be here if it weren't for her.

Not wanting any personal contact at the moment, he folded his arms in his lap and listened to Thorn explain the procedure.

When he slid Sophia a sidewise glance he saw that her face was as rigid as a sheet of glass, and just as transparent. She didn't like this.

"We'll start with a thorough physical," Thorn said. "Dr. Miguel Valero has just arrived from Baltimore so he'll be able to do that now."

"Okay," Jonah agreed. He glanced at Sophia. "I guess you have to wait outside now."

After she left, Valero came in and introduced himself. Then Jonah stepped into a dressing room, stripped and put on one of those white gowns that open down the back.

IN THE LOUNGE, Sophia tried to sit still with her hands wrapped around a mug of tea. Unsuccessful, she finally had to get up and pace the room.

Kathryn Kelley came over to her. "I know this is hard for you."

She nodded.

"Do you want to talk about it?"

Sophia glanced around. There were other people in the room, and she didn't want to bare her soul in front of them.

"Let's go down to the sunroom," Kathryn suggested.

She scuffed her foot against the floor. Although she wanted to talk about her and Jonah, she didn't want to get into anything too revealing. But who was she kidding? She'd already revealed a lot. Maybe Kathryn could give her some insights.

"Okay."

They walked down the hall to a room with huge windows and skylights. It had a warm, earthy scent, coming from the pots of plants that filled the room. Color came from orchids, bright tuberous begonias and cyclamens. But there were also large ficus and dracaena trees, many sparkling with tiny lights in the darkness. They gave the setting an ambiance that Sophia would have appreciated if she hadn't been so strung out.

She sat down in a wicker chair, staring out onto the grounds where spotlights illuminated the well-tended gardens.

"I guess they put a lot of money into keeping this place up," she remarked.

Kathryn sat in another chair. "Some of the researchers have to stay here for weeks, and Cameron Randolph wants to create a comfortable environment for them."

"I see."

The conversation died away, and they sat in the darkness for several minutes until Kathryn gently suggested, "Why don't you tell me what's been going on."

"You already heard Jonah's account of our adventures."

"Right. Your adventures. The guy version. Very fact-filled. But I didn't hear anything about your emotions. Or his."

Sophia grimaced. "He's pretty uptight."

"And you're being pretty guarded." Kathryn spread her hands. "We don't have a lot of time for extended therapy here. If you tell me what's going on with you, I'll give you my considered opinion."

Sophia lowered her eyes. "I guess the bottom line is that I told him I was in love with him, and he didn't bother to respond."

"I guess that was hard for him to deal with—under the stress of running for your lives."

She nodded. Then, because she had nothing to lose, she said, "I had a crush on him in high school. I know he liked me, too, but he always acted like he thought he wasn't good enough for me. In the past few days, we've talked about his life back then. I didn't realize how hard it was."

"How does that make you feel?"

"Like I was too self-centered to notice."

"Or he hid it from you. Probably not just from you—from a lot of people."

She huffed out a breath. "I think you're right. But it doesn't make me feel good about myself back then."

"But you did reach out to him?"

"Yes. Just before he left for Fort Benning, I brought him to my house when my parents were in Europe. I mean, it wasn't a kid sneaking around," she added quickly. "I was nineteen. And he was a couple of years older. I never forgot that night, and I think he didn't, either. Later, when I got married, it didn't work out partly because I kept comparing my husband to Jonah. And partly because George married me for my money, I think."

"That's a lot to walk around with."

"Yes. But Jonah and I are both a lot more mature now. I think we could build something together. But he won't let me close." She heaved a sigh. "Well, he let me get physically close, but he's guarding his emotions."

"You might have gathered from his behavior that he feels like he's damaged by what happened to him in the bunker and in Afghanistan," Kathryn said.

"Yes," Sophia answered in a small voice, still unwilling to meet the other woman's eyes.

"So perhaps he's putting your relationship on hold until he feels he has more to offer you."

She gave Kathryn a fierce look. "He doesn't have to do that!"

"But he's a proud man, and he obviously feels he has to."

Sophia had thought of his pride, too. Now she felt as though a giant hand was squeezing her lungs. Nervously, she looked

toward the door. "That physical is taking an awful lot of time."
As she thought about the implications, she stood.

"Show me where to find the lab."

"That may not be a good idea," Kathryn murmured.

"Show me!"

"All right."

She followed Kathryn down the hall, silently urging her to
move faster.

They stepped into the medical wing of the building again.

Kathryn pointed. "Down the hall."

Sophia hurried toward an area where white light shone
through an interior window. As she got closer, she could hear
voices. When she drew abreast of the window, she looked
through and gasped.

She'd thought Jonah was only going to have a physical. At
least, that's what he'd let her believe. Now he was lying on a table
with his eyes closed, apparently unconscious.

She took in the scene in the blink of an eye. He was dressed
in a white gown, his arms and legs strapped to the table. That was
bad enough, but then she saw that electrodes had been attached
all over his head.

"No!" she cried out.

Through the window Thorn looked toward her. And when she
ran to the door, Kathryn was right behind her, grasping her
shoulder to hold her back.

## Chapter Seventeen

"No. I've got to…"

She didn't know what she intended, but she had to do something.

She'd known it. Known it on some unconscious level she hadn't been able to deal with.

Jonah made his own plans. He was going ahead with this with no regard for her.

When Kathryn's hand tightened on her shoulder, she whirled to face the other woman.

"Were you in on this? I mean keeping me talking in the sunroom so he could…could take a chance on frying his brain?"

"No, I wasn't." Kathryn stared into the room. "This is as big a surprise to me as it is to you."

Sophia clenched her hands at her sides. She wanted to hit someone, Jonah, actually.

Through the window she saw Thorn and another man watching her.

"Who's that?"

"Dr. Valero."

"So he okayed this?"

"I assume so," Kathryn answered.

"I want to talk to him, or Thorn."

Kathryn cleared her throat. "I'm sorry, but I think it might be dangerous to interrupt now."

Sophia glared at the other woman, but she silently acknowledged that the assessment was probably right. If she'd gotten here a few minutes earlier, she might have been able to make Jonah stop and think about the risk he was taking.

Now it was too late.

She stayed where she was with her hands clenched at her sides as Thorn fiddled with the damn equipment, then walked to a computer console and started typing on the keyboard.

Sophia tensed, then gasped as Jonah's body jerked. Kathryn leaned toward her. "I know it looks scary, but Thorn knows what he's doing. This isn't the first time he's used this procedure."

"Easy for you to say," Sophia snapped. "They're not experimenting on the man you love."

"They did," she answered.

Sophia whirled around, her eyes questioning. "They did this to Hunter?"

"Worse."

Outrage bubbled inside her. "How could it be worse!"

Kathryn continued quietly, "Hunter was a clone—raised for a suicide mission. He didn't even have a name. I met him because I was hired to…socialize him, but I had no idea what I was getting into."

Sophia gasped. "You're kidding."

"No." Kathryn held her gaze steady. "A lot of the people who work for Randolph and Light Street have been through some pretty harrowing experiences. We're a very resilient group."

Sophia swallowed. "I guess," she murmured.

"As you can imagine, Hunter and I had a lot to deal with after we escaped from the secure facility where they were training him to be an assassin. So I'm pretty in tune with what you're going through."

Sophia nodded, hearing the strong emotion in Kathryn's voice. Kathryn and Hunter had gotten through the worst, but that was in her past. Jonah was strapped down to a table right now. And the sight was pretty frightening. What if this "treatment" damaged his brain?

Beside Sophia, Kathryn whispered, "I think it's working."

"How do you know?"

"See his eyes moving under his lids. He's dreaming."

"About what?"

"I hope we'll find out."

JONAH TRAMPED forward through a kind of twilight country where the landscape was a series of indistinct blobs. Where was he? Afghanistan… West Virginia… Thailand?

No, Thailand wasn't real. It had never been real. Those were memories Dr. Montgomery had fed him. He knew that much.

The thought of the doctor made him wary, and he glanced over his shoulder. There was nothing behind him but more indistinct shapes. When he faced forward again, he saw light ahead of him.

The closer he got, the more he was certain it was Afghanistan, and the more his chest tightened with determination. He had to go back there to find out what was so bad that he had no memory of the events.

He was almost there. Except that he seemed to be standing behind a translucent curtain. Beyond it he could see the brown hill he remembered.

He stepped toward it, and then a shadow crossed his path. It resolved itself into a man—Dr. Montgomery.

"Stay out," the doctor ordered.

Confusion swirled in his mind. "You want me to go back there. That's what the bunker was all about."

"You can't go until I say you can. Not until I'm beside you, recording your experiences."

Anger surged, and Jonah answered with a curse. "The hell with you."

He felt Montgomery grabbing the back of his shirt, trying to keep him in the twilight.

He yanked himself free, and suddenly he was through the curtain, walking toward the village. He wasn't alone. Shredder was beside him and Hall and the other men who were part of the rescue operation.

Rescue operation! Yeah, that's what it was. He remembered that now.

They'd come in by helicopter, landing twenty miles from their intended destination to keep the mission secret. They were wearing native garb, not their usual combat outfits.

This was an important covert operation, and Colonel Luntz didn't want anyone getting wind of their presence in the area.

The Colonel had sent them here to pick up Jamal Al Feisal, an al-Qaeda defector with valuable information.

Sweat trickled down the back of Jonah's neck and down his face. He wiped his brow on his sleeve and looked to his left.

"You think somebody's following us?" he asked.

"Naw. It's your nerves jumping," Hall answered. He always had been overconfident.

"Yeah, but I can't shake the feeling that there's someone out there."

He reached in his pocket and pulled out the map they'd been given. There was supposed to be a village just ahead. But he didn't see the damn place.

The map was a piece of crap. Maybe the whole mission was a piece of crap. They'd already made a couple of detours around huge rock formations that weren't supposed to be there.

Shredder looked at him. He could tell his buddy was thinking the same thing. But they couldn't go back. Al Feisal was too big. If they left him here, he'd be killed by his own people who thought he was a traitor. He was counting on Colonel Luntz to hold up his end of the bargain.

Too bad the unit was on radio silence so they couldn't ask for directions.

"What do you think?" Jonah asked.

"Let's see what's over the next ridge," Shredder said.

They plowed ahead, and when they climbed the rise, they could see houses in the rocky landscape. So was this the place where they were supposed to pick up Al Feisal?

If so, there was supposed to be a contact in the village, a young guy who had helped the Americans before—assuming the map was correct and it was the right place.

They started down the slope toward the houses, moving cautiously.

From the village, he heard the sound of music. A foreign melody that could have been a dance tune played on flutes and percussion instruments.

He stopped short.

"Something wrong?" Hall asked.

"I don't know," Jonah answered. But he was lying. The music told him that the bad part was coming. The part he didn't want to remember. He felt his head whipping from side to side as he tried to get away. Still, the images pummeled him.

The gunfire. Men lying on the ground, some of them already dead, some of them screaming in agony.

Through the memories he heard a voice. "Easy."

Jonah gasped, his body jerking as blinding pain shot through his head.

His eyes flew open, and he felt himself shaking as he looked around in disorientation. A moment ago, the Afghan landscape had been spread out in front of him in vivid detail. Now it had vanished.

Not just the landscape. The ambush.

He struggled to grasp on to that memory, but it flitted out of his mind, and he cursed.

When he tried to sit up, he found he was strapped down to some kind of table. He screamed, then screamed again as he looked wildly around, trying to figure out where he was. All he could think was that Montgomery had him. Montgomery was doing something horrible to him.

He heard a door bang open, heard a woman's voice call his name, her panic leaping toward him.

Turning his head, he saw her rush forward, her face contorted with fear.

"Jonah. Oh God, Jonah."

He stared at her. Who was she? Why did she care about him? Was she one of the villagers?

No. He could tell she was an American from her clothing and from her golden hair.

For a terrible moment, he was lost as he scrambled for context. And then memories came flooding back. "Sophia?"

"Yes!"

"What are you doing in Afghanistan?" he asked, even when he knew that the question had no meaning. He wasn't in Afghanistan. He was…

The location wouldn't come to him.

Her voice captured his attention again. And her beautiful eyes—so full of fear. "You know me?" she asked with such urgency that he could tell the answer was important to her.

"Yes. But I don't understand where we are," he managed to say.

"We're at the Randolph Security research facility—in western Maryland."

He tried to take that in, but it wasn't making any sense. He stared at her helplessly.

She leaned over him, loosening the straps that held his hands and feet. He was aware of activity behind him. Turning his head, he saw a man removing some kind of wires from his head.

He stiffened. "What's going on?"

"Jonah, everything's okay. You're okay," she said, but he could tell from her voice that she wasn't sure it was true.

When he tried to leap off the table, someone pressed a firm hand to his shoulder.

"The music," he gasped out, panic almost closing off his windpipe. "The music."

"What music?"

"The woman was playing it. No wait—this time the woman wasn't there." He blinked in confusion, trying to sort through what was real and what wasn't.

Sophia leaned over him, then brushed her mouth gently—so gently—against his. "Let's start with the good part. Do you remember making love with me?" she asked softly.

A sizzle skittered over Jonah's nerve endings.

"Making love with you," he murmured against her lips. "Yes, I remember that." His gaze burned into hers. And he did remember. Making love all those years ago, and a few days ago. It had been wonderful back then, and just as wonderful when he'd found her again.

He stared at her in amazement. "I remember," he said, just to make sure it was true—and that she understood how much it meant to him.

"Good."

He dragged in a breath and let it out. "I mean, not just us. I remember the assignment in Afghanistan." He felt as though a terrible weight had been lifted off his chest as relief flooded through him. "I remember. I can tell you about it."

## Chapter Eighteen

Sophia's look of relief almost took his breath away.

"Why is that so important to you?" he murmured.

"Because it's important to *you*."

When she reached for his hand and linked her fingers with his, he held on tight.

But there were still questions whirling around in his mind. "Why couldn't I remember the mission? What the hell was wrong with me?"

"Did you feel betrayed by Luntz?"

"Yes!"

"That's the key, I think. You had to drive Afghanistan from your mind because the whole thing was such an enormous betrayal of everything you believed in—everything you'd devoted your life to. He was in your chain of command, but he sent you to do something bad."

"We didn't know it was bad."

"Of course not."

His gaze turned inward. "Is that why Montgomery cooked up that false story about Thailand? Because he knew I couldn't let myself go back to Afghanistan?"

"I think so. He knew that was safer for you than reality. He gave you memories that were more acceptable."

When he grimaced, she continued. "Probably he started with the diplomatic mission. And when you wouldn't cooperate, he added the part about you going berserk and endangering everyone—to give you more reason to cooperate with him."

"How did he do all that?" he asked, the question making his mouth so dry that he could hardly speak.

"With mind-altering drugs."

"Just drugs?"

"And techniques to induce the behavior he wanted. Then he started digging back into the Afghanistan mission. Maybe he planted the idea that it was just a dream."

He thought about that. "Yeah, that makes sense," he answered, although deep in his consciousness he felt a small scrap of doubt. He banished it.

"I kept dreaming about it. But not what really happened. I guess I couldn't face it—even in a dream."

"So you twisted it into something else."

"You'd think I'd make it into something good."

She gave a hollow laugh. "Apparently, you couldn't go that far. But when you put Lieutenant Calley into the middle of it, you had someone to blame."

"Yeah." He heaved in a breath and let it out. "So—am I really suffering from post-traumatic stress?"

"Well, not in the classic sense if you list all the symptoms."

"Is that good or bad?"

She shook her head. "We don't need to fool with labels now. Let's just deal with what we have."

He considered that, then said, "Okay. I guess the most important thing is telling you the real story."

"Yes. I want to hear it. But maybe you'd be more comfortable if you put some clothes on first."

He looked down, seeing he was wearing one of those hospital

gowns that left your ass flapping in the breeze when you walked around. "Right. Let me get dressed."

A man came forward. Dr. Valero. And Jonah realized that he and Sophia had been engaged in this private conversation in front of an audience.

"How do you feel?" the doctor asked.

"Fine," he said automatically.

"I want to check you over. Then you can meet with the rest of the team."

Jonah might have objected, but he was pretty sure the doctor was going to insist. So he went back to the exam room, where he got a medical okay.

Half an hour later, dressed in jeans and a Ravens T-shirt, he sat in a comfortable lounge area. Sophia was beside him, holding tightly to his hand, while other men and women were grouped on chairs and couches around him. Apparently they all knew him. Only when Sophia introduced him to each of them, did they became familiar to him.

As he spoke to them, flashes of memory came back to him like waves lapping at a beach when the tide comes in.

These people worked for the Light Street Detective Agency and Randolph Security. They were more than coworkers. They were good friends who were always there for each other.

They'd sent Sophia and a man named Phil Martin into the back door of the bunker to get him out. And now he was going to tell them why he was being held at the bunker.

Some of the pieces were still missing, but he was pretty sure the rest would come back to him when he started talking.

Clearing his throat, he said, "The whole thing was Colonel Luntz's show. He had us detailed to a covert operations unit. Then he created a false mission—something he could put down on the record. He sent us to pick up a guy named Jamal Al Feisal, who was supposed to be an al-Qaeda defector. He said that the guy had information valuable to the War on Terror. But all of that was a lie. He was really an Afghan warlord who was funneling millions of dollars in illegal drug money to Luntz. Well, not just that. Antiquities. Gems and gold that were illegal to export."

Hunter looked as if he was taking that under advisement. "How do you know the cover story was a lie?" he asked. "I mean, how did you get the real story?"

"Because I heard the attackers talking when they thought they'd killed us."

"Back up," Cameron Randolph said. "Who thought they'd killed you?"

"A rival faction. They had a couple of American guys with them. Nixon and Fromer. I guess they were mercenaries who were hired to protect the opium. They were speaking to each other in English, which is why I could understand them."

Sophia made a small sound.

"What?"

"When I hypnotized you, you thought a man named Fromer was at the briefing with you. He attacked you."

"Yeah, he attacked me. But not at the briefing. In Afghanistan. I guess I still had that jumbled up."

She nodded.

"They were working for a rival warlord who was getting ready to kill Al Feisal. He'd found out he was in danger and wanted out. That's why he contacted Luntz—who sent us in to rescue a guy we thought was a defector. They shot us all, including Al Feisal."

Jonah had to stop and swallow as the gruesome scene came flashing back to him. The blood, the heat, the flies. The shock and horror had penetrated his soul. He hadn't been able to deal with the enormity of it, so he'd turned it into something else.

But he remembered everything now.

He kept his voice even when he said, "The rest of the unit was dead, and the bad guys thought I was, too. I was shot and bleeding, and I had blood on me from the other men. Then, when it got dark, somehow I got out of there and into a cart that was leaving the area. I ended up in a friendly village and was eventually turned over to the Americans. The villagers thought they were doing the right thing, but Luntz swept in and got custody of me. As far as anybody knows, I'm still missing in action."

"And Luntz is afraid you're going to tell what happened to the rest of the team," Sophia said.

Jonah laughed, and it wasn't a pleasant sound. "He could have killed me right away if that was all he wanted. He was going to do that to shut me up, but before he could, I got out of there with the money and the treasure. He wants to know where I hid it."

A babble of voices broke out in the room. When it calmed down, Sophia asked, "You know where the loot is?"

"Yeah, I do," he said with satisfaction. Then he realized the victory wouldn't do him much good. "He's going to hunt me down and kill me. And kill you," he said in a strangled voice.

"No," she answered.

"He's desperate, and he's got a private army working for him. Guys who were in the military. Badass guys. I'll bet a lot of them were dishonorably discharged, but he offered them a job because he valued their skills."

"Why didn't he send his own men to pick up Al Feisal?" Hunter asked.

"Because he couldn't get them certified. Remember, they were already known troublemakers. So Luntz had to work through official channels."

"Couldn't they use false names?" Sophia asked.

"Not with their fingerprints on records."

"He thinks he's got the upper hand, but we've got the resources to stop him," Cam said in a hard voice. "So let's start planning our operation. Starting with a visit to his house."

Jonah looked around at the men and women in the room, seeing the determination on their faces. He remembered that he hadn't trusted them. Now he understood that they were his friends—and the key to whether or not he could rescue Sophia from the nightmare he'd dragged her into.

SOPHIA WAITED with Jonah and some of the others for a report from Max Dakota, who had taken a team to the Luntz house. While she waited, she made her own plans.

The bad news came when Max and the team returned by helicopter. "He's gone. Cleared out."

As she and Jonah exchanged glances, Max continued talking. "The place is empty. We got inside, and there's no indication of where he went."

"Great," Jonah muttered.

"My guess is that you shook him up with that invasion into his turf. He's obviously worried that you'll come after him again, and the next time, you won't bother with talking."

"Funny thing," Jonah answered. "It sounds like a Mexican standoff. I can't find him as long as he's hiding, and as long as I hole up here, he can't find me." He glanced at Sophia, who was sitting beside him on the sofa. "Or you, either."

She nodded tightly, waiting for Max to finish his report. When he was done, she cleared her throat.

"What?" Jonah asked.

"I have an idea."

"You mean like when you thought of strolling into his house and telling him you were a psychologist working with me?"

She kept her gaze steady. "No. This time you're the one who has the major role."

"Let's hear it," Hunter said.

She continued to stare at Jonah. "What if you can convince him you're no threat to him?"

"Like how?" he demanded.

"Like you're in such bad mental shape that you can barely function. You escaped, and now you don't know what the hell to do. You're paranoid. You think everybody's after you. You just want this nightmare to be over." She gulped. "I've left you high and dry because you're so whacked up that…that you attacked me. All you want is to get back into the bunker so Montgomery can make the pain and confusion in your head go away. But you don't know how to find the front entrance to the place. So you're out in the West Virginia woods, looking for the back way in, through the cave. But you can't find that, either."

She dragged in a breath as everyone in the room stared at her.

"It might work," Jed Prentiss said.

"But it's dangerous," Sophia admitted. "You'd have to…" She stopped and started again. "Jonah, you'd have to make yourself a target."

"Whatever it takes, it's worth it," he growled. "Pretending to be a mess isn't going to be so difficult."

She took her lower lip between her teeth. She wanted some private time with him. She knew he wanted her, physically, just as she ached to kiss him. Just a kiss—if that was all he was willing to give her.

But he had built a wall between them again. She understood why. He still thought he was dangerous. He didn't know what the future held for him, and he was afraid to let himself reach for happiness. There was nothing she could do about any of that—not until Luntz and Montgomery were rounded up.

While all that churned in her head, Cameron began speaking. "Okay, let's get the sting operation set up."

"We should start with a phone call," Jed added.

"To his house, even when we know he's split?" Jonah asked.

"Yeah, because *you* don't know that. And there's no evidence that we were there."

"Did he have security cameras?"

Max laughed. "His security system had a malfunction."

Jonah grinned, and Sophia could see that he liked these people and trusted them.

"Before you make any calls, we have to decide what you're going to say," Sophia told him.

She'd thought that might give her some time alone with him while they did some planning. But he thwarted her plans by quickly saying, "You and Kathryn can coach me."

JONAH WAS dead tired.

He, Sophia and Kathryn had found a smaller room where they could work on his monologue. Now, two hours later, he figured he was as ready as he'd ever be. And Randolph Security was also ready with a special hookup to a prepaid cell phone.

With Sophia beside him, he walked back to the lounge. Jed, Cam and Kathryn gathered around him as he dialed the number.

As he expected, he didn't get Luntz himself, only voice mail. When it beeped, he went into the monologue he'd rehearsed.

After a string of fiery expletives, he finally got around to saying something semicoherent.

"You're not there! Where the hell are you? I need to talk to you." He stopped and swallowed. "Oh yeah, right. Forgot to say. This is…this is Jonah Baker," he said, his voice making it clear that just saying his name required a tremendous effort. "I…I'm in trouble. And I need your help. Please, call me back. The number is…."

He gave the number of the cell phone, then gulped. "I feel like my brain is on fire. Do you know what that's like?" he shouted, then added another string of curses for good measure. When he was finished with the blast, he apologized with a shaky, "Sorry."

He paused for effect, then went on. "Listen, I can't hold a thought for more than a few seconds. Please, I need some more of that medication I was taking. That made me feel better. I want to hook up with Dr. Montgomery, but I don't know how to reach him, and I don't know how to get back to the bunker. I went down to West Virginia and started searching, but I'm so turned around that I can't find my ass with a flashlight."

He glanced at Sophia.

"Good," she mouthed.

He gave her an apologetic look. "That chick who got me out of the bunker—she left me high and dry. Just because I roughed her up a little. She said I was crazy as a bedbug, and she couldn't take it anymore. She told me I needed medical treatment. I didn't want to believe her, but now I think she's right. Only the bitch took off while I was sleeping and she didn't even leave me with any meds," he whined, going back to the previous topic. "I can't handle this. I need help. If Dr. Montgomery is willing to take me back, I'll do anything he wants. He said hypnosis could help me. I didn't want to do it before, but I'll try anything. Please, call me back." He gave the number again, then hung up.

"Now we wait to see what he says," Cam said.

"And if he doesn't respond?"

"Then we go to plan B."

"Which is?"

"We'll figure that out if and when we need to."

Jonah leaned back and closed his eyes. He was completely wiped out.

"You should get some sleep," Sophia murmured.

He didn't have the strength to object.

"When Luntz calls, you can talk to him and we'll monitor the conversation," Cam said.

Jonah nodded, then looked around. "I don't even know where I'm bunking."

"I'll show you," Jed said.

He followed Jed down the hall to a room with a double bed. He half expected Sophia to barge in after him, but when she didn't appear, he figured she was giving him some space.

He fell onto the bed with his clothes on and was instantly asleep. This time, there were no dreams.

SOPHIA PACED back and forth in the hall. She knew Jonah had to sleep. But she also knew that he could have asked her to share the room with him.

She walked past his door and stopped, thinking that she could go in and lie down next to him. That way, he'd have to speak to her when he woke up. Or maybe not. Maybe Luntz would wake him up, and then he'd have to be on his toes.

Other people at the complex passed her in the hall. She tried to return their greetings, but it was difficult to focus on anything else besides Jonah.

He had been through a horrible ordeal, and it wasn't over yet. In fact, she'd suggested that he put himself in danger. But she knew it was necessary and not just for the reason she'd given everyone. Montgomery and Luntz had damaged Jonah's self-esteem. They'd used him in the worst possible way, first by sending him on that mission and then by screwing with his mind. They'd intended to get what they wanted out of him—then kill him.

Well, he'd escaped from the damn bunker. Now he needed to show them that he was the winner in this situation.

Once he proved to himself that he was back in charge of his life, they could deal with their relationship.

What if Jonah walked away from her again when this was all over? That would be like a kind of death.

She clenched her fists. It was all she could do to stop herself from charging into his room, waking him and demanding that he tell her what he intended when he had his life back.

But she knew he wouldn't give her the answer. Not yet.

Was he smart enough to realize that the two of them belonged together and had always belonged together? Or would he throw their future away because he thought he wasn't good enough for her?

All she could do was pray that he came to the right conclusions.

# *Chapter Nineteen*

Jonah sat up with a start.

Something was jangling in his head.

Music?

His stomach clenched.

No. Not music. It was the cell phone ringing.

It must be Luntz. Nobody else besides Sophia had the number.

Glancing at the clock, he saw that the colonel had waited six hours before responding.

He rubbed his eyes and cleared his throat. Then, feeling better than he had in days, he picked up the phone. "Colonel Luntz?"

The man on the other end of the line drew in a quick breath. Jonah could imagine him rearing back. "How do you know who this is?"

"I didn't know." He lowered his voice. "I was praying you'd call me back."

"Where are you?"

He gave a hollow laugh. "I'm not *that* stupid. I'm where you can't find me—unless I want you to."

"I wouldn't count on that."

Jonah glanced up as Cam came into the room and sat down in the easy chair. Sophia stood in the doorway. They'd both been waiting for the call, too. The phone volume was turned up so both of them could hear the other end of the conversation.

Jonah swore. "If you can trace this call, maybe I should hang up."

"No! Wait. We can help you," Luntz said.

He shoveled despair into his voice. "Sometimes I think nobody can help me."

"The problem is, that girl screwed with your mind."

"You said it!"

"I can take care of her for you."

"Like how?"

"She left her fingerprints in the bunker. We know her name. She's Sophia Rhodes. She's supposed to be working for the Howard County Mental Health Department." He made a deprecating sound. "But she took a leave of absence to go and get herself into trouble. Who's she really working for?"

Jonah's skin went cold. He glanced at Sophia, knowing his expression looked sick. "She didn't tell me."

"And now she's disappeared," Luntz said. "We know you grew up in the same town. Ellicott City, Maryland. Is she your lover? Is that why she got you out of that bunker? And how did she do it?"

He glanced across the room at Sophia. This was a development he hadn't expected. "She said she vacationed in the area. She knew about the cave entrance."

"Ah. But how did she know you were there?"

"She didn't tell me. I think someone paid her to do it."

"How do I know you're being straight with me?"

"What do I have to do to convince you?"

"Meet me at the location of my choice. Come alone."

Jonah heaved in a breath and let it rush out. "How do I know I can trust you to help me?"

"You don't."

His curses ranged over the phone line. "I don't know if this is such a good idea. Maybe you're after me, too."

"And maybe I'm the only one who can save you," Luntz said.

"Screw you," Jonah answered and pressed the "off" button.

He looked at Cam and Sophia. "He'll call back. He wants me bad."

"Yeah," Cam agreed.

Jonah pressed his hands against the mattress to keep them steady. He was shaken, and he knew Sophia could see his reaction. The conversation had taken more out of him than he'd expected.

Sophia took a step into the room, and he stiffened.

"Are you okay?" she asked.

"Yeah," he answered, praying it was true. He had to do this. It was the only way they could get Luntz.

Was he up to playing his part? He had to be. Yet a tiny splinter of doubt had lodged in his brain. He had remembered Afghanistan. Everything should be okay. Yet he was afraid to trust that the rest of it was going to work out.

"Maybe you want to take a shower and shave," Sophia murmured.

"Do I look that bad?"

"You look like you'd feel better if you cleaned up."

"Yeah. But I'd better not shave. I've got to look like a wreck when I meet Luntz."

"Right. I wasn't thinking about that. Take a shower and change your clothes. Then we can eat."

"If I can swallow anything."

Sophia laughed. "They made you some chicken soup. That should be easy enough."

She was right. He did feel better after showering, brushing his teeth and eating. The soup was good. But he had to wait three long hours for that bastard Luntz to call back. And he couldn't stop himself from pacing back and forth across the lounge as he waited.

When the cell phone finally rang, he snatched it up. "Hello?"

"I have a counteroffer," Luntz said.

"It better be good," Jonah growled.

THE NEGOTIATIONS went on for the next two days, with Jonah coming across as a man at the end of his rope, a man who was willing to do anything to stop the pain in his head. But still a man who was afraid to show himself.

He was pretty sure Luntz didn't trust him, but he was the key to a great deal of money and treasure that the colonel thought he deserved. Too, Jonah had information that could hang Luntz, which meant the colonel had to deal.

Jonah said he was afraid to travel far, making it sound as though he was deteriorating. If the colonel didn't get to him soon, he would be too whacked out to do anyone any good.

They finally settled on a meeting place in the Prince William National Forest.

The Light Street team scoped out the area, then dug themselves in where they couldn't be detected. By the time Luntz sent his men to reconnoiter, it looked safe.

Or that's what Jonah was hoping by two in the afternoon—the appointed meeting time—as he waited on a gravel road by a sign that said, "For law enforcement purposes, the right side of the road is West Virginia and the left side is Virginia."

Jonah turned in a full circle, his eyes probing the forest, wondering if one of Luntz's men was already watching him.

He looked like a man who'd been sleeping rough. His beard was growing out and he had on grubby clothes. He also had a Glock in his hand—for all the good that was going to do him. Still, he knew that the nut he was portraying would never come unarmed.

There was no time for self-doubt now. They had planned every detail of this operation.

Of course, Luntz was probably thinking the same thing.

Jonah heard tires crunching on gravel a long way off, and his hand began to shake.

*Good,* he told himself. That would add to the verisimilitude.

Two Land Rovers pulled up on the Virginia side of the road. The windows were all darkly tinted, so that he couldn't see inside. He stood with his heart pounding as the back door of one opened, and Luntz got out. He wondered how many other men were in the vehicles.

"Major Baker."

"Colonel Luntz."

"Good to see you again."

Jonah shifted his weight from one foot to the other.

"You asked for my help."

"Yes."

"Put the gun away."

"I feel more comfortable holding it."

"You understand why I don't."

Jonah shrugged.

"Let's go to a safe place where we can get you the help you need."

Jonah looked around at the forest. "This is a safe place."

The colonel followed his gaze. "Not for me. But if you insist, we can secure the area." He waved his hand, and more car doors opened. Six men in blue uniforms got out. Men he remembered seeing in the bunker. They stood with their backs to the cars, automatic weapons pointed in all directions.

"Ambush," Jonah shouted, taking a step toward the side of the road, cowering back, making it look as though he was terrified out of his mind.

"Take it easy," Luntz ordered.

"Afghanistan was an ambush."

"What the hell are you talking about?" the colonel demanded.

"You wanted Jamal Al Feisal to give you the money from the opium trade, but another warlord was way ahead of you."

Luntz goggled at him. "How do you know about that?"

"I remembered. That was the thing I didn't tell you." He giggled like a maniac about to crack in two. "That's what you really wanted, wasn't it? The money."

"You couldn't have remembered. That was part of the conditioning for the mission. Your memory was supposed to be wiped the moment you finished. That's why we had to dig it out of you."

Jonah stared at him, then swore. "You screwed with our minds before we left for Afghanistan?"

"Yes," Luntz hissed.

As he stood there—vulnerable and exposed—Jonah scrambled to assimilate this new information. Sophia had suggested a perfectly reasonable explanation for what had happened to him. She'd thought he couldn't deal with what had really happened. But there had been no way for her to know what Luntz had actually done to him and the other men.

"I didn't finish the mission," he croaked, giving a reason for why his memory had suddenly come back.

"Who else did you tell about this?"

Jonah stared at him. The man had already implicated himself in something illegal, but Jonah wanted enough on tape so that the Defense Department would have the information they'd hired Light Street to obtain.

He was planning what he was going to say next when a sound stopped him dead. From inside one of the Land Rovers he heard musical notes. An Afghan dance tune, such as they might play at a village celebration.

"No," he shouted, clapping his hands over his ears.

Dr. Montgomery stepped out the back door, holding a metal box. He closed the car door behind him and thrust the box toward Jonah. It must have had some kind of recording device inside, because when the doctor turned a dial, the music grew louder, faster.

"No," Jonah screamed, going down on his knees.

Luntz turned to the other man. "You said it would disable him, but it's hard to believe it works. How could music do that?"

"Part of the treatment." Montgomery laughed. "A nice little method for controlling him. I implanted the trigger when I gave him the false memories of the assignment in Thailand. Whenever he heard the music, he'd go incoherent."

"But he remembers Afghanistan."

Luntz came forward and took the gun from Jonah's hand, tucking it into his own belt. Jonah looked up at him with watery eyes. He tried to crawl away, tried to get away from the tune.

But Luntz stepped in front of him, blocking his escape. "Too bad I didn't have that music box when you came to my house. This charade would all be over by now. We'd have the money, the treasure, all of it. We could already have gotten rid of you."

Still down on his knees, Jonah fought for coherence. "You killed those men," he shouted. "The other men on the patrol with me. You killed them."

Luntz waved his hand. "Collateral damage. That wasn't how I planned it. You were supposed to come back, then forget about what had happened—and Dr. Montgomery would give you false memories. I had no way of knowing another warlord was going after Al Feisal." He came down beside Jonah. "I'd like to kill you now. But not until you tell me where you hid the damn loot."

Jonah struggled to make his mind work, despite the jangly tune threatening to blot out coherent thought.

"We'll get the information out of you, then we'll put you

out of your misery. Where is the money and the treasure?" Luntz demanded.

"Screw you."

Montgomery brought the music box closer to Jonah's head, and he screamed in pain.

The doctor's leering face loomed over his. "Are you trying to pull something on us?"

Fighting for control of his tongue, Jonah managed to get out one syllable, "No."

And then above them, the treetops exploded in a series of concussions that blotted out the sound of the music.

The men in blue uniforms were instantly on the alert, raising their guns, pointing toward the threat in the trees. But they didn't know that the concussions were no more than fireworks.

A diversion.

"What the hell…" Luntz shouted and jumped back, heading for the safety of the car. But Montgomery had closed the door when he got out. As they fought to open it, Jonah scrambled to his feet and leaped forward, grabbing for the box.

The tune almost robbed him of thought. He had only one goal—making it go away.

Montgomery flailed at him with one hand, grasping the box tightly with the other.

Jonah snatched at it, the music making his movements jerky. It felt as if hours were dragging by, though it was probably only seconds.

Finally he wrenched the box from the doctor's grasp, threw it to the ground and stamped on it with his boot, crushing the thin metal sides.

The music stopped, and the blessed relief was like the sound of angels' wings beating around him.

Then, from the woods, a curtain of choking smoke enveloped all of them.

The men around Jonah began to cough. Jonah himself was immune because of an injection Thorn had given him earlier.

He knew he had won. Still, he needed the personal satisfaction of socking Montgomery on the jaw, watching the man gasp in pain as he went down.

The colonel had gotten the car door open. Jonah yanked his hand away and whirled him around.

"Damn you," Luntz shouted between coughing fits. "Damn you. It was a perfect plan to bring the money and the treasure back to the U.S. And you spoiled it."

More men poured onto the road, the men from the Light Street Detective Agency and Randolph Security, but there were others with them. Operatives from the special Department of Defense unit that had asked them to find out what kind of illegal operation Luntz was running in Afghanistan.

They were the ones who hustled the colonel, Dr. Montgomery and their men into secure vehicles that pulled up behind the Land Rovers.

Sophia came running out of the woods, and he knew she must also be protected from the smoke. Still he gasped when he saw her.

"I told you to stay out of this," he choked out.

"I wasn't going to leave you here alone."

He looked from her to the receding vehicles.

"It's really over," she said, punching out the words. He swung back toward her, his face registering disbelief.

"It's over," she said again. "Believe it."

"Did you hear the part about their planting a trigger in our minds before we left?"

"Yes. I'm sorry. I didn't think of anything like that."

"Who would?" He considered that for a moment, then

laughed. "I guess they thought they were so clever—giving us a command to forget. Then the mission blew up in our faces, and they got me back. But they'd made it so I couldn't remember."

"So they had to set up the whole bunker scenario to pry the information out of you." She took his arm and led him away from the smoke to a shelter that the Light Street men had commandeered. Part of a Defense Department installation that had been built in the area years ago, it was underground, dug into the forest floor and invisible unless you bumped into one of the ventilator shafts.

Cam Randolph had studied the area, which was why he had suggested the meeting place, and Jonah had knocked down all of the colonel's proposals, insisting that he had to meet on this road.

Sophia switched on the light, then closed the door behind them before turning to face Jonah.

"Are you all right?" she asked.

"Yes."

"That music! Oh God, that music. You were talking about music when you woke up from Thorn's treatment. I should have paid attention to you."

His face turned grim. "You couldn't know Montgomery was using something like that. I didn't understand the implications. Nobody could," he said, softening his voice.

She kept her gaze on him. "In case you haven't figured it out, the bad stuff is over," she said, her tone very sure and authoritative.

He stared at her, trying to take it in. Was he really free from the nightmare of Afghanistan? The nightmare of the bunker? Of Montgomery's diabolical interrogation methods?

She kept her gaze fixed on him. "So you have no more excuses."

"Excuses for what?"

"For turning away from me," she said in a strangled voice. "To make it perfectly clear, I mean, either you admit you love me and we go on to make up for all the years we lost, or you walk away because you can't stand the idea of the two of us being happy together."

He swallowed hard, then said the words. "I love you."

"Thank God."

"But I'm no good for you," he said, in the spirit of full disclosure.

"Of course you are. You were ten years ago and you still are. We loved each other back then, but neither one of us could admit it. And since then, no relationship has ever worked for either one of us."

He silently nodded in agreement.

"We belong together. We always have."

"Yes, but you have a PhD. I'm—"

"A patriot. A man with his feet on the ground. A man with values I admire. A man with courage and strength."

"You make me sound like…a saint."

She laughed. "Hardly. Thank the Lord, you're a human being, with flaws. But I know your strengths are greater than your weaknesses. I knew that back in high school."

"You might be overestimating me."

"No. As you said, I'm a trained psychologist. I'm a very good judge of people. So stop looking for excuses to back away from me. "I love you, but I can be objective."

He stared at her. "But—"

To keep him from saying anything he might regret, she reached out, brought his head down to hers and pressed her mouth to his. When she did, all the emotions he'd been holding in check exploded through him.

It was as if someone had finally given him permission to be happy. Or maybe he'd given himself permission. Finally, after all the years of missing her.

She was in his arms and nothing was keeping them apart. Not anymore. He kissed her with all the passion that had been pent up inside him since they'd arrived at the Randolph research facility. She kissed him back with the same intensity, her mouth moving under his, opening so that she could taste him with greedy enthusiasm.

As her hands stroked over his back, down his body, pulling his hips against hers, his did the same, touching her everywhere he could reach.

The need for her burned through his blood, and he was about to raise his head and look for a place where he could make love with her when the door slammed open.

They both looked up in shock to see Max Dakota staring at them. He grinned.

"Sorry."

Jonah stayed where he was, his arm protectively around Sophia.

"Cam wanted to make sure you were okay."

"Yeah, I am."

"We've moving out. Unless you want to spend the night here, you've got five minutes." Max grinned again and stepped back outside.

Jonah dragged in a breath and let it out.

Sophia laughed. "I can walk in front of you, if you want."

"I'll be okay in a minute—as long as I know there's a bed waiting for us in the very near future."

She laced her fingers with his. "Oh, yeah."

He dragged in several more breaths and ran his free hand through his hair. "Okay. Let's go."

The rest of the Randolph–Light Street group was waiting in several vehicles that had been hidden in an underground garage.

"Ride with me," Cam Randolph said.

They both climbed into the back of his SUV, and he pulled away.

"We were a little worried back there," Cam said, "when Montgomery pulled his stunt with the music box."

"Luntz wasn't going to kill me until I told him where to find the money and the treasure."

"Luckily, because he sure looked like he wanted to."

Sophia winced.

Cam drove through the national forest, then headed north.

"You did a fantastic job of getting Luntz and Montgomery to talk. The military will be able to go back to the area where he sent you and get the loot. And the villagers can verify what happened. So it's over for you, except testifying at the trials."

"Yeah," Jonah murmured. "And I'd say my military career is over, too. It may be illogical, but I'll never trust the chain of command again."

"But you trust us," Cam said.

"I know that now," Jonah answered.

"Good. Because I was hoping you'd join our organization. We've got a lot of ex-military and ex-spies. You're just the kind of guy we need, and you obviously fit right in."

Jonah took a breath. "I…"

"You don't have to give me your answer right away. But I did talk to the Defense Department, and they're willing to expedite your army discharge—if that's what you want."

Jonah felt his chest expand. "I don't have to think about it. I know the answer. I felt at home the moment I sat down and started talking to all of you."

"Good."

Sophia gripped his hand tightly. When he looked at her, she smiled.

He pulled her close, and she leaned her head against his shoulder.

"It's really over," she murmured. "I can hardly believe it."

"No, it's just beginning," he said, feeling happier than he had since the night he'd first made love with her. There was so much he wanted to say to her, but not in front of anyone else—even his friends.

Still, he knew by the warm look in her eyes that she was on his wave length. As soon as they were alone, he was going to start making up for all the lonely years. She grinned at him and he grinned back, sure that the rest of his life would be so much different from anything that had gone before—except for that one glorious night that had kept him going for all these years.

"Happy?" she whispered.

"Yes."

"Well, I predict you ain't seen nothin' yet."

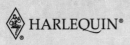

HARLEQUIN®

*American ★ Romance*®

# CATHY McDAVID
# Cowboy Dad

## THE STATE OF PARENTHOOD

Natalie Forrester's job at Bear Creek Ranch
is to make everyone welcome, which is an
easy task when it comes to Aaron Reyes—the
unwelcome cowboy and part-owner. His
tenderness toward Natalie's infant daughter
melts the single mother's heart. What's not
so easy to accept is that falling for him means
giving up her job, her family and the only
home she's ever known....

**Available August
wherever books are sold.**

## LOVE, HOME & HAPPINESS

     HAR75225

# REQUEST YOUR FREE BOOKS!

## 2 FREE NOVELS
## PLUS 2
## FREE GIFTS!

### Breathtaking Romantic Suspense

**YES!** Please send me 2 FREE Harlequin Intrigue® novels and my 2 FREE gifts (gifts are worth about $10). After receiving them, if I don't wish to receive any more books, I can return the shipping statement marked "cancel." If I don't cancel, I will receive 6 brand-new novels every month and be billed just $4.24 per book in the U.S. or $4.99 per book in Canada, plus 25¢ shipping and handling per book and applicable taxes, if any*. That's a savings of close to 15% off the cover price! I understand that accepting the 2 free books and gifts places me under no obligation to buy anything. I can always return a shipment and cancel at any time. Even if I never buy another book from Harlequin, the two free books and gifts are mine to keep forever.

182 HDN EEZ7  382 HDN EEZK

| | | |
|---|---|---|
| Name | (PLEASE PRINT) | |
| Address | | Apt. # |
| City | State/Prov. | Zip/Postal Code |

Signature (if under 18, a parent or guardian must sign)

Mail to the **Harlequin Reader Service:**
**IN U.S.A.:** P.O. Box 1867, Buffalo, NY 14240-1867
**IN CANADA:** P.O. Box 609, Fort Erie, Ontario L2A 5X3

Not valid to current subscribers of Harlequin Intrigue books.

**Want to try two free books from another line?**
**Call 1-800-873-8635 or visit www.morefreebooks.com.**

* Terms and prices subject to change without notice. N.Y. residents add applicable sales tax. Canadian residents will be charged applicable provincial taxes and GST. Offer not valid in Quebec. This offer is limited to one order per household. All orders subject to approval. Credit or debit balances in a customer's account(s) may be offset by any other outstanding balance owed by or to the customer. Please allow 4 to 6 weeks for delivery. Offer available while quantities last.

**Your Privacy:** Harlequin is committed to protecting your privacy. Our Privacy Policy is available online at www.eHarlequin.com or upon request from the Reader Service. From time to time we make our lists of customers available to reputable third parties who may have a product or service of interest to you. If you would prefer we not share your name and address, please check here. ☐

HI08R

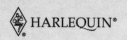

# HARLEQUIN®

# INTRIGUE®

## COMING NEXT MONTH

### #1077 THE SHERIFF'S SECRETARY by Carla Cassidy
Sheriff Lucas Jamison and secretary Mariah Harrington had always butted heads. But with her son's life in danger, Mariah trusts the sheriff to uncover a kidnapper hiding in their peaceful community—no matter the secrets revealed.

### #1078 DANGEROUSLY ATTRACTIVE by Jenna Ryan
With a killer terrorizing police detective Vanessa Connor, Rick Maguire was assigned to protect her. But the enticing federal agent had to lead her further into danger if she was ever to be safe again.

### #1079 A DOCTOR-NURSE ENCOUNTER by Carol Ericson
A relationship between Nurse Lacey Kirk and Dr. Nick Marino had always been expressly forbidden. But nothing could keep them apart amidst a string of deadly cover-ups and patients with secret identities.

### #1080 UNDER SUSPICION, WITH CHILD by Elle James
*The Curse of Raven's Cliff*
Pregnant and alone, Jocelyne Baker believed her love life had been cursed. Yet only fate could have led her into the arms of Andrei Lagios. The cop wore away her defenses, even as the rest of the town grew wary of Jocelyne's return to town.

### #1081 BENEATH THE BADGE by Rita Herron
*The Silver Star of Texas: Cantara Hills Investigation*
Nothing mattered more to Hayes Keller than the badge he wore. But while protecting heiress Taylor Landis, the heart of a real man in need of a good woman was soon exposed.

### #1082 BODYGUARD FATHER by Alice Sharpe
*Skye Brother Babies*
Garrett Skye had a habit of taking on bad assignments, and now he was on the run. But he wasn't willing to leave his baby daughter behind, and that meant taking a stand with teacher Annie Ryder at his side.

www.eHarlequin.com

HICNM0708